Side Chicks Catch Feelings Too

A NOVELLA BY **ASHLEY TE'ARRA**

SIDE CHICKS CATCH FEELINGS TOO

© *2019*

Published by **Miss Candice Presents**

All rights reserved.
This is a work of fiction.
Names, characters, businesses, places, events, and incidents are either the products of the author's imagination or used in a fictitious manner.
Any resemblance to actual persons, living or dead, or actual events is purely coincidental.
Unauthorized reproduction, in any manner, is prohibited

ASHLEY TE'ARRA

NOTE FROM THE AUTHOR

My first novella is here, baby! What a blessing... to have yet another book out!

I remember the days where I would dream of having a novel with my name on the bottom of it. Now, I have FIVE!

Don't ever doubt what God can make happen for you. Dreams do come true; you just have to be willing to put in the work to turn them into a reality. Once you take the first step, he'll guide you through the rest.

I have so many more steps to go, but I'm thankful for the ones I've taken so far and will only continue to keep going!

Thank you to my super-boss publisher, Miss Candice, my mother, Beverly, and my sister, Brianna, and my beautiful readers for their outpour of support. Also, showing appreciation to my aunts, uncles, cousins, and friends; you know who you are!

This has been one journey to remember and cherish. I will forever.

Love, Ashley Te'Arra

CHAPTER ONE

CAMISHA "MISHA" ATKINS

My legs were falling weak and shaky, pussy becoming so wet that I could literally feel the moisture sticking to my plump thighs. I couldn't take any more of the foreplay, dammit. I just wanted him, *all of him*. I began rubbing the back of my barefoot right heel against his strong back, hoping that he'd take the hint. He didn't, though. Instead, he kept going, and going, and going. He'd been head-first in my cat for the last twenty minutes—licking and sucking on my vaginal lips—flicking my pink pearl with every inch of his long, wet tongue. The arousal heightened by the minute. Placing my French-manicured fingertips on the back of his shiny, black bald head, I pushed him deeper and deeper into my sticky treasure box. The more I creamed, the more he ate, and he was determined to slurp every bit of it up. I don't know what turned me on more: knowing that my warm juices were trickling through the hairs of his thick, perfectly-trimmed beard, or the fact that I was practically sitting on his tongue, letting his mouth be a table for my gushing liquids of passion and pleasure. Whatever it was, it made me realize just how much I fucking loved this man.

As he capered around my opening with his mouthpiece, he continued letting his broad shoulders serve as a support system for my two legs, which were thrown over them so effortlessly, as if I wasn't a solid 350 pounds, with thighs thick enough to save many lives.

"Mhmmmm." He tongue-fucked me at a fast pace, wrapping his arms around my big ass and squeezing it up into his scrawny hands like a newly-bought bag of marshmallows. He was skinny, but with that skinniness came the strength of a man who'd been putting in some heavy weight-lifting. I was a whole lot of woman, but somehow, someway, he handled all of it, and I mean *all* of it.

Lying back onto the bed, staring up at the ceiling, I wondered what I'd done to deserve such a good man. They say nobody's perfect, but, hell, Cameron Dargan was, without a doubt, perfect for me. Who would've thought that the guy stocking the shelves with Coca-Cola drinks would become my best friend, my confidant, my fuck buddy... shit, my man. Certainly, not I. You see, at first, I didn't think Cameron was the cutest, and, to my eighteen-year-old self, back then, that meant more to me than having a nice personality. Sad, but it was the damn truth. I usually preferred my men caramel and a lot younger, but he was as black as the night's sky and old enough to have been my almost-forty-year-old brother's grade-school bully. Let's not get started on his height either. The dude was barely 5'7". My best friend, Mimi, called him a Taye Diggs reject, but I beg to differ. It was just something about Cameron. Something that made my toes curl and my clit jump in excitement. Any form of contact with him would make my kitty feel like it had a mind of its own. Not long after dating, he drew me in. For a while, he chased, but eventually, he caught me, and dammit, I can't say that I regret it either. Love really does conquer all.

"You want some of this dick now?" Cameron asked.

He arose from in between my legs, letting them down slowly. Before I knew it, he was approaching me, face first, kissing me dead in my mouth. I smiled in between smooches, honored that he'd granted me the opportunity to get a taste of my sweet nectar. I wrapped my soft, moisturized lips around his tongue, damn near sucking it dry. He giggled at my aggression, which came as a shock to him, being that I was as delicate as a flower outside of the bedroom. Well, at least, I tried to be. The phrase "a lady in the streets and a freak in the sheets" described me to a T. I guess that's just the Leo in me; once you let this lady lion out of its cage, it's hard to keep her tamed.

"Put it in me, baby," I demanded seductively, staring

directly into those beautiful hazel eyes of his. The eyes, they were what always got me with Cameron. He could undress me with those in a heartbeat, and I'd be face-down and ass-up, on all fours, ready to risk it all for him. That's just how sex-crazed that man had me. His pipe and head game were unmatched. I hadn't dealt with anyone quite like him, which could've been due to the fact that, aside from Cameron, I'd only slept with one man in my entire twenty-five years of living.

At fifteen, I had a quickie in the bathroom of my high school, with the popular kid, Brandon Johnson. I had been crushing on that dude since middle school. Little did I know... he'd invented the term "fuckboy" long before I'd even known what it meant. Turns out, he had a whole girlfriend and baby on the way, and he even admitted that he only fucked me to make me "feel good about myself." The fuck?! But that's how these niggas will do you. They'll play on your fucking emotions... only because they think that they can, and by you being so easy and hard-up to give them what they want like I was, you prove them right. If I knew then what I know now, I would've let Cameron be my first. But, shit, each and every time that Cameron and I made love, it felt like the first time all over again.

Letting our lips depart from one another, he took his

nine-inch wand and placed it at my entrance. At this point, I was hungry for him to be inside of me. I wanted him, more than ever; I was craving him. Instead, he enjoyed teasing me. He patted his seemingly humongous dipstick on my twat. The sound of our private parts hitting against each other made me yearn for him uncontrollably. I felt like a crackhead needing her fix; he was my drug of choice.

"Stop playing with me, Cam," I said, as I rolled my eyes, pouting like the brat I had always been—especially when it came to something that I wanted. I took my two hands and began caressing my double-d-cup breasts, massaging them. I thought that maybe that would get him excited enough to shove it in, but he began rubbing them, too. While it brought me great satisfaction to see him cupping my jugs and nibbling on my nipples like a baby's bottle, I grew annoyed by his stalling.

As he swept around my areolas with his tongue, I looked down and reached my hand in between his legs, blindly searching for his hardened manhood. Once found, I stroked it slowly with my right hand. I was making him feel so good that it was hard for him to concentrate on juggling my titties. He came up for air, biting his lip and fastening his eyes shut. He hated looking like a bitch, but right now, he was—and I was enjoying the hell out of it.

He removed my hand, instantly ramming his curved

dick deep inside of me. I gasped in disbelief. Though I was familiar with his stroke game, it still caught me by surprise. I was a big girl, and I knew that I could handle it; it'd just take a couple of seconds for me to get readjusted. I tried scooting up into the bed, attempting to let some of the pressure off of me down there. Cameron damn sure wasn't having that, though. I was aggressive in bed, at times, but he was aggressive all the time. What Cameron wanted to do he was going to do. And, at this moment, he wanted to fuck the shit out of me, so that's what he was going to do.

He pulled me back to the edge of the bed, bending his knees so that he could get better and deeper strokes. That man fucked me so hard that I was ready to repent, and he fucked me so good that I was willing to wash all of his clothes, his wife's and kids' clothes.

Shortly after I met Cameron, he told me that he was married, but I still agreed to get to know him, all based on the fact that he was supposedly "about to get a divorce." However, here we are, seven years later, and a divorce hadn't even been filed. Deep down, I knew that he wasn't going to get that divorce. I wasn't willing to let go, because if I let go, I'd risk the chances of her winning him, for good, and I wasn't ready to make that sacrifice. Yeah, they were married on paper, but when it all boiled down to it, I knew that, in

Cameron's head, they'd been divorced. His heart belonged to me. He was only holding on for the sake of their two kids, Kennedy and Jaxon. Had it not been for him wanting to keep his family together, he would've left a long time ago. He would've because he loved me. To be frank, he was in love with me. Just as much as I was in love with him.

With my arms pinned behind my head, he did the same with my legs—pinning them so far back that they were now spread wide open into the air. I was more flexible than most, and that's what Cameron liked. He wanted me to feel everything, and he wanted to see everything. Shit almost felt like I was lying across a doctor's table, getting operated on, and I was a complying patient.

"Ahhhh!!!"

I held my legs up, already growing tired and short of breath. It just felt too damn good to stop now.

"Fuck this pussy, baby! Yes, daddy!" I moaned and groaned, while he showed no mercy.

He was murdering my pussy with every stroke, but he was so focused on doing my box right that he didn't even realize it. Tears welled in my eyes, as I felt myself on the verge of releasing. Happy tears laced with love.

I yelled out in fulfillment. Meanwhile, Cameron said nothing. He was, what I liked to call, a silent fucker. He barely made any sounds, but I think I'd just about made enough for the both of us.

"I'm cumming! Shit, I'm cumming!" I yelled, looking up at him, finally letting my ankles fall back into his hands.

"Yeah, come on, Misha. Come on!" he coached me, knowing just the words to say, how to say them, and what to do to keep me cumming.

He pulled out of me, and within seconds, my juices were spewing everywhere. He jacked his dick, watching me cum. I knew he wanted his; it was all over his face. And, as his woman, it was my duty to make sure that he got it.

"Yeah, squirt that shit in my mouth," he said, kneeling at my pussy, with his mouth hung open.

"Fuck!" I yelped, giving him exactly what he asked for. "Get up."

I beckoned him to come around to the side of the bed. He stood up, dick still fully erect and condom off. Now on my stomach, I crawled to the side of the bed, placing my mouth in front of his lengthy, girthy rod. I licked the tip, loving the sight of him going crazy just by witnessing the wetness of my tongue. I wanted to tease him, just as he had teased me.

"Fuck, I need you, Misha! I need you right now! Suck this dick, baby. Yeah, suck it!" Cameron yelled.

He was the loudest I had ever heard him. He took his

hand and placed it on the top of my head. I flipped my eighteen-inch Havana twists to the side, making sure that I had no interruptions or interferences while getting the job done. I was very confident in my head game. Cameron was the first and only man I'd ever done it on, and he had no objections, whatsoever. In fact, he'd even said that I was better than his wife, Dahlia. I wore that as a badge of honor.

Putting him through no more torture, I went to town on him—sucking, slurping, and bobbing. I wanted him to feel how much I appreciated him and I was willing to show him just that. After five minutes, he was already shooting off on the pinnacle of my breasts. Once finished, he went into the bathroom and grabbed warm towels for us to clean up with. That's what I always loved about having sex at Cameron's house; we had the bathroom and the bedroom in one place. Where I come from, bathrooms in bedrooms were only for the rich.

"Dahlia's coming home with the kids tomorrow, so I won't be able to see you again, at least, until the weekend," he said, turning the bathroom faucet off.

I pulled the covers up over my naked body. Positioning myself upward, I laid my back against the headboard and mumbled, "Cam..."

"I know, Misha, but just hang on. I promise, all of this will be behind us in no time, and it will be you and me living in our own house, together."

"You've been saying that for, what, seven years?! When am I going to be put first? You said that I'm the woman you want to be with, so what's the fucking hold up?!?!" I yelled, raising my voice. I was tired of his sorry-ass excuses.

"Right now, I've got a lot of shit on my plate. Just be patient with me, babe." He stood in the doorway of the bathroom, propping his hand up on the frame of it.

When I was eighteen, I never would've thought that I would meet a man ten years older than me and fall in love. I was fresh out of high school, getting ready to go off to school at Troy University that August. A committed relationship, of any sort, was nowhere near my fast-ass mind. I was boy-crazy and excited about college life. I wanted out; I wanted to have fun. Coming from a strict household, freedom always seemed so far out of reach. I was the only girl out of five children. The baby, at that. So, my parents were very protective of me. My whole life, I had basically been dependent on them. I never worked; my older brothers took over that load. They were responsible for helping my parents finance the household. So, I had it easy. Too easy, actually. It wasn't that I didn't want a job, it was that I wasn't allowed to get one. Mama was too busy teaching me how to be a wife that she forgot to teach me how to be a woman. She never taught me how to fend for myself, instead of always having to depend on a man like she'd done most of her life.

My mom and dad had been together since high school. They got married a year after graduating. My oldest brother just turned thirty-eight. You do the math... a long time, right? So, she was forced into that lifestyle early on—cooking, cleaning, and obeying. That's just how she was raised and taught, though. Mama came from a long line of Southern-bred, submissive women. Anniston, Alabama, to be exact. All of them believed in catering to their husbands and letting him be the leader of the household. Women were supposed to be in the house, doing and saying whatever the hell their husbands wanted them to do and say. It was forbidden for a woman to actually have a life and a mind of her own. So, when I grew older and wanted both, my parents weren't having that. Well, technically, Daddy was the only one stern in his demands, but if Daddy disagreed, Mama couldn't dare agree. He made the decisions for them.

Fortunately, I didn't let their decisions dictate the way that I lived my own life. I owed that all to Cameron because, months into courting, he freed me from the prison that I once called home and moved me into an apartment. It was furnished and paid for monthly, by him. Things were getting pretty serious between us, and he wanted to make sure that I was happy, in all areas of my life. This was physically, mentally, emotionally, and financially. He knew that I wasn't happy living up under my parents' roof, and he made sure that he did everything that he possibly could to provide me with what I needed. Cameron even went as far as giving me weekly allowances to ensure that I was good. Hell, you'd think that I'd feel bad, being that he had a whole family to feed, but I didn't. I felt that I deserved just as much as the wife deserved, especially since I'd dedicated myself to him and stayed loyal.

Besides, as much as she tried to turn the other cheek, Dahlia couldn't possibly think that Cameron was being faithful to her. We hooked up every other weekend when she was conveniently out of town. It seemed to me that she knew exactly what was up and was either too dumb or in love to leave him. Maybe she just didn't want to be faced with the harsh reality of her husband, her high-school sweetheart, fucking and catching feelings for a young, fat bitch. A young, fat bitch who could probably turn a backflip better than she could a piece of bacon. She probably couldn't stand it and was too afraid to speak up about it. She was a successful interior designer, so I don't think could've been about the money. It came off more like she wanted him just to say that she'd succeeded at keeping him.

SIDE CHICKS CATCH FEELINGS TOO

Out of the seven years that I've known Cameron, I could count on one hand the times I've crossed paths with Dahlia. Not that I preferred to anyway. One time at Cameron's job, where we both coincidentally showed up to treat him to lunch, and the other time at Kennedy's kindergarten graduation, that I was invited to. Oh, yeah, he was that bold. He said he told her that I was his cousin, but what woman with good sense would believe that? He was such a bad liar. To be real, I didn't like the bitch, and I wouldn't have cared if he broke the truth to her. I couldn't seem to understand why she had chosen to hold on to the fantasies and false hopes that Cameron had sold her, especially when we all knew that their relationship was simply a ship that had sunken long ago. She could've been only trying to get it to stay afloat for the sake of security, which was something that Cameron offered both of us. Mentally for her, financially for me. If her foundation was to crumble, he probably had the necessary tools to put it back together.

However, it wasn't the security that had me under his spell. It was his ability to make me feel like I meant something to somebody, and his ability to love and caress me like no other man ever could. This man meant everything to me, and I'd been fighting so hard to show him just how badly I wanted to mean *everything* to him... without Dahlia. I loved him with no limits, no boundaries, no regards. I didn't give a fuck about who tried to get in the way of what we had. Cutting my parents off should've been enough for him to see that. When everyone else was against us, I was for us... always had been, and always would be. I only wanted the same in return.

"I'm trying, Cam. I really am. I just can't wait for the day where it can just be you and me. Fuck all of this extra shit." I looked ahead, daydreaming of the future.

"It will be. You just have to trust me." He re-entered the bedroom, hovering over me as his minty breath beat against my eyelids. "All I've ever wanted was you, baby. You know that. This divorce shit gets hectic when you have kids involved."

"We can start our own family." I peered up at him, cuffing his head in my two hands, as I leaned up on the California King Bed. "Your kids and our kids can become one. Blended families are the new thing."

His buff chest met my face and he planted his muscular arms on each side of me. He looked like a chocolate Adonis. To be in his mid-thirties, he didn't look a day over twenty-eight.

"In due time," he whispered, gently kissing my lips before handing me the towel. His lips were dark as fuck but pink at the center. I loved that shit. "Here, clean up. I'm going to hop in the shower. Are you sure you don't want to join me?"

"Yes, I'm sure. I'm good. I'll shower when I get home."

He nodded, heading to the shower as if my heart hadn't just been broken into a thousand pieces.

This was the part of the dream that I'd always hated—having to wake up and realize that the fairytale had suddenly come to an end. Shit was real again, and, for me, it was always hard to accept what was real, particularly, when it came to him and I. I was so lost under the sea of Cameron's love that I forgot about the complicated world that awaited above us. The reality was, legally, he was someone else's, and he'd never be mine, wholeheartedly. Not until he ended things with Dahlia. But the question was... did he really want to? I was exhausted from playing number two to a man who had always remained my number one. Why hadn't I walked away earlier? Was I wasting time? It sure felt like it, but I always gave our situation the benefit of the doubt. *Maybe he does want to be completely done with Dahlia, but she won't let him*, I convinced myself. Then... I would think about what Mimi often told me, "Can't no woman make a man do something he really doesn't want to do." *Maybe he wants to be there*, I thought. I could never admit that, though, even if the signs were there.

The vibration of the bathroom's door shutting, startled me, interrupting my thoughts. The sound of the shower water hitting the bathtub filled my ears until Cameron's iPhone began to buzz. I thought about picking it up but quickly decided to ignore it instead. I felt uneasy when the buzz started up again, and again, and *again*. I knew that, whatever it was, it had to be urgent. His phone had never rung like this. At least, not while I was around.

Shifting myself to the other side of the bed, I grabbed the phone from the nightstand and noticed six missed calls from Dahlia. However, it was the text that I saw that damn near knocked the wind straight out of my body and made my heart nearly jump from my chest to my feet.

Dah-Dah: *I'm pregnant.*

CHAPTER TWO

CAMISHA "MISHA" ATKINS

"Oh, so this is what it is!?" I yelled, bombarding my way into the bathroom to confront him. "That bitch is pregnant?!"

"What are you talking about?" Cameron ducked, afraid that I would uppercut him like I've done on other occasions. "Can't you see that I'm trying to get dressed, woman?"

"*This* is what I'm talking about! You see this shit! She said she's pregnant, Cameron!" I held up his phone, pointing at the recent text message. "I thought you said you weren't fucking her anymore! You told me that you hadn't had sex with her in almost a year!"

"Give me my phone!" He latched on to my wrist, trying his best to yank that iPhone X away from me. "Misha, we can talk about this! Just calm down!"

"We can't talk about shit! Answer my question, Cameron! Have you or have you not been fucking this bitch, Dahlia?!" I screamed at him, mushing his head the opposite way.

"You act like she's not my wife!" he justified, taking a towel from the rack to wrap around his waist. "Yes, we fuck, but it's only when we have to."

"Have to?!" I laughed to keep from crying. My blood was boiling. "Are you hearing yourself right now?! You're full of shit." I dropped his phone inside of the toilet and pressed the flusher.

"The fuck you do that for?!" He was mad. Real mad. "Bitch, you're going to pay me my money for that!" he yelled, standing over the toilet.

"First of all, who are you calling a bitch?!" I yelled as I turned around, in his direction, smacking him upside the head.

"You need to chill, Misha. Keep your hands to yourself!"

"I need to chill? You know what, lose every fucking memory of me, including my number! I'm gone out of your life forever! I can't take this anymore! I can't!" I broke down in tears, grabbing my clothes from the floor and stuffing them into my duffel bag. "I hate you! And that baby can die for all I care! Trashy-ass hoe."

That was cold, but the thought of him having a baby with Dahlia repulsed me. He'd given her what I'd been begging him to give me for almost two years: his seed. I wanted to have a child with him and start our life together, but he was so stuck on the one he'd created with her that he couldn't even begin to start one with me. A year into our relationship, I got pregnant, and unbeknownst to Cameron, I went to the abortion clinic. It was childish and dumb, but I got an abortion. I did it because I feared that if I kept it, he'd walk away from me. He had already expressed his views on having a child with his 'mistress.' He was against it. But I regretted that shit—and I still do... to this day. Which is why I want a chance to make it right. I wanted the blessing of being the mother of his child. It's okay if it's his wife, though, right? She gets to have the babies and the big house? But what about me? You'd think the two kids Dahlia already trapped him with would've been enough. She had them before I met Cameron, so I couldn't really trip over that. But another one? Oh, I damn sure could trip over this. I couldn't believe that I had fallen for his lies. I felt so stupid, so useless, *so dirty*. How did I let him take advantage of me for so long?!

"You knew what it was!" he hollered, following me back into the bedroom. "I'm a married man; you knew what you signed up for when you got with me."

"*I* knew what it was? *I* knew what it was?" I repeated with emphasis on the 'I', jabbing into his chest with my index finger. "No, nigga, *you* knew what it was! You sold me a damn dream! And I bought that shit like a dumb ass."

"How did I sell you a dream, Misha? How? Tell me

that!" He yelled, as he forcefully moved my hand out of his face and sat on the bed.

"You told me that you were going to divorce her and that *we* were going to be together!" I reminded him of the bullshit he'd been brainwashing me with, resting my hands on my wide hips. "That's the dream that you sold me!"

"Misha..." He took his strong arms and pulled me in by my love handles.

I pushed him away, fighting the additional tears. "Don't Misha me! You led me to believe that you guys were on the verge of separation and sleeping in different beds! Yet, y'all made a baby in the same exact bed you just ate my pussy on!" I was so disgusted that I couldn't even see straight, and my stomach churned.

"It was actually in the guest bedroom," he smart-assed. "That's where me and her had sex."

"Are you fucking serious right now? Everything is a joke to you, Cam! Everything!" I yelled, throwing punches everywhere he could catch them. "I hope you die. I swear to God!"

"Stop hitting me, Misha! You know I didn't mean it like that!" He guarded himself, with a smirk sitting at each corner of his juicy-ass lips. This nigga was sick. It was becoming clear to me that all of this shit was just a big turn-on for him.

By this time, my chest was heaving and hair messier than it was when he was pulling on it from the back. I just needed to get home, shower, and pray him out of my mind and soul, even though it was going to be hard. I felt like a whore, *his* whore. Like I was a toy that he only picked up after he'd put the others down. Did he ever really love me? Or was telling me he loved me just an easy way to fuck me and manipulate me? Maybe I needed him more than he wanted me. Right now, hating him was less complicated than admitting that. Despite everything that just transpired, I still loved him. That wouldn't change overnight, and I was crazy to expect it to. Feelings are real, and soul ties are ever more real. Unfortunately, with this man, I had both.

I didn't give him another second to make another excuse; I packed my shit and left. I cried the whole way home, speed-dialing Mimi. I needed someone to bring me back from the ledge I was so close to jumping off of. If I could've, I would've killed his ass and not thought twice about it. Killing him would be easier than living with the hurtful revelation that Dahlia was the chosen one and that I was just convenient. Him impregnating her said more than his words could ever say. Every time we had sex, we had to use protection since I refused to get on birth control. Mimi's sister was on that shit, and it ended up fucking her system up.

When I refused to use birth control, Cameron grew extremely careful when it came to not ejaculating inside of me. Boy nearly threw my ass to the ground—dead in the middle of me riding him—one day, just to make sure of it. I guess he forgot that women can get pregnant from pre-cum too. He believed that having a kid would make things difficult. Make what difficult? Us? Our 'relationship?' Something that he swore up and down that he wanted? Something that, when I threatened to walk away the first time, he got on his knees and pleaded for? Never mind how difficult he'd just made things for me. While I was off smelling the roses in La La Land, he had been laying up and letting loose with her. Someone he supposedly couldn't stand the sight of.

"Fuck, Mimi! Pick up!" I yelled. Any other time, my best friend would answer on the second ring. I kept calling and it kept going to voicemail. Eventually, I gave up.

The drive from Cameron's home on Leighton Avenue to Fox Valley Apartments seemed like the longest one ever. I lived near Lenlock. It's a small community on the outskirts of Anniston. I pulled into the parking lot, cut the ignition to my silver 2008 Chevrolet Malibu off and just sat there. My thoughts were racing, as was my heart. Surprisingly, it was still beating, even after being snapped in half. I got inside and peeled my garments off, put my hair in a low bun and popped my red bonnet on. Walking by the mirror, I doubled back, noticing how unattractive the lumps, rolls, and marks on my thighs were making my 5'1" body appear. Normally, Cameron would trace my stripes, squeeze my coffee-toned legs, and tell me how beautiful I was. That's what I'd miss most; the constant affirmation that my figure was still fabulous, regardless of the size of the circumference. It's funny how the same person who helped me see the value of my worth was the same one devaluing and diminishing it. Would I ever be worthy of being someone's all? Or would I always be an option?

    Staring at the wall clock, it was now nine o'clock on this rainy, Saturday night. I ran my fingers down the bridge of my nose, gaping at the face of my Android phone, which was tossed at the foot of my bed. I hoped that Cameron would call, but he didn't, and I'd left him hours ago. A sorry wouldn't fix it, but it could pad my shattered heart for a second or two. It could take this pain away temporarily and let me know that he cared and that he really hated to hurt me. I waited for hours for that phone to ring. I showered, untwisted my Havana twists, pin-curled my real hair, ate a pint of ice cream, and watched five re-run episodes of *Martin* and yet still, he didn't call. Mimi called though.

    "I called you earlier. Where were you?" I asked her

when I picked up, brushing dandruff from my stretchy, green halter top. My twists had been up for a month, so I was relieved to have them out. They were itching my scalp like crazy, and I needed a wash. But I was too discombobulated to even set an appointment with my beautician.

"Sucking dick. What's up?" she vulgarly joked. "I'm kidding. I was at the park with the kids. Jeremy went to go play some stupid-ass golf with his buds."

"I think Cameron is done with me," I stated, as I grabbed yet another pint of Bluebell's butter pecan ice cream from the freezer. I then walked into the living room and climbed on the sofa. "And I have no choice but to be done with him, too."

"You should've been done with him. I told you he was going to end up dumping you before you dumped him. You weren't strong enough to, so God did it for you." I could hear baby Asia crowing in the background, along with three-year-old Madison, screaming, "Mommy!"

"His wife is pregnant," I blurted, then I ate a spoonful of butter pecan ice cream. "I don't know what to do, Mimi."

"Leave his ass where you found him! With her!" she scolded me, right before chastising her daughter, Maddy. "Madison, if I have to tell you one more time to get down from that damn bookshelf, it's about to be World War Three in this piece."

She'd been telling me to kick Cameron to the curb since she'd first found out about our situation, which was a week into it. I couldn't not tell her. In the beginning, it was actually a thrill for me. Knowing that I held enough power to possibly take a man away from his home enticed me. Clearly, I was mistaken. I hate that I'm just now realizing that shit all of these years later. Shame on fucking me.

"That's easier said than done. What did you do when Tyson left you? Need I remind you?" I asked, throwing her ex-husband up in her face, licking the back of my spoon.

She'd been screwing him and the other bitches he'd coerce her into inviting into their bedroom for years until she caught him and one of the threesome chicks in bed together... alone. That's exactly why I said I'd never do that shit. Well, that, along with the fact that I have zero interest in women. Anyway, they stopped fucking for like a month, then she went back to him and got knocked up with Madison. They tried the happy-family thing for like a month or two, but he ended up leaving her pregnant, swollen-footed, and heartbroken. You would've thought that she'd be done with his ass after that, but the rollercoaster continued, and baby number two came.

Having babies won't keep a man who doesn't want to be kept, and she quickly learned that. He'd pop in to play with her emotions when he felt like it but would always find a way to pop back out. Though she eventually moved on, it took her a while to get over what Tyson had done. So, I couldn't understand why she'd even fix herself to think that getting over Cameron would be like slicing cake.

"Yeah, I cried over that shit for a few months, but I bounced back and bossed the fuck up. Now, look at me. I'm happy, in a new relationship, and totally fine with co-parenting. Just be glad you dodged that bullet."

"What bullet?" I bent over to pick up the pecan that'd just rolled to the floor.

"Having his babies. Don't get me wrong; Maddy and Asia are my world. Buuuut, because of them, I have to deal with their ain't-shit daddy for the rest of my life," she blatantly griped. "It is what it is, though. I can't change it now, but if I could, you better believe that I most definitely would. Jeremy is more of a father to them than Tyson could ever be."

"You're right, but this really hurts, Mimi," I said, feeling bloated as I sat the carton of ice cream on the end table beside the couch. "A part of me wants to talk to Dahlia, woman-to-woman, while the other part just wants to ruin Cameron and everything attached to him."

"Baby, don't even bother getting revenge. Trust me, it

ain't worth it. You could shoot a nigga in his right leg, and you know what he'll do?"

Rubbing my forehead, I let out, "What?"

"Hop back to that other bitch with the left one." We both fell out laughing. Nothing about this matter was humorous, but I have never needed a cackle as much as I needed that one. This is why Mimi would forever be my sister. "So, don't sweat that shit. Get yourself together. You'll be okay, and that's a promise."

"Thanks, Mimi. I really appreciate your effort to cheer me up."

"I got you, always," she assured. "Now, let me get off this phone before these kids tear my house up."

"Alright, talk to you later."

After we hung up, I went to the refrigerator and got the leftover bottle of Barefoot Sweet Red Wine that I'd purchased from Walmart a few days ago.

The mood that I was in was fucked up enough to make me drink it straight from the bottle.

My mind kept going over everything. I felt cheated, foolish even. I couldn't go out sad like this. The more wine that I drank, the more clear the solution to all of this had become. It was time to get that bitch, Dahlia. Once and for all, she needed to be shown the exit out of Cameron's life and mine. Hell, Cameron played with my heart, so maybe it was time to play with hers. And I wasn't playing nice. One of us would have to lose, and it'd be her.

Let the games begin.

CHAPTER THREE

CAMERON "CAM" DARGAN

"Why didn't you answer my text yesterday? I saw that you read it." Dahlia stood at our marble-top island in the kitchen, chopping vegetables for the salad she was making. "Are we going to talk about this or what?"

It hadn't even been a full hour since my wife and the kids' arrival, and she was already grilling me like she was my probation officer or something.

"I destroyed my other phone by accident yesterday. You just came in this morning, Dah," I replied, going through my back-up cell. "I don't mind talking about it now."

"What happened to it?" she fished, raking the tomatoes to the center of the cutting board with a large, butcher knife. "Couldn't you have called me from this phone that you're on now? Your wife literally texted you and told you that you're having another child, and you come up with some weak-ass excuse as to why you couldn't respond?"

"I took it in the bathroom with me, dropped it down the toilet while trying to respond to your message," I said, somewhat telling her the truth. "I couldn't get to this phone. Look, that doesn't matter. What matters is this elephant in the room."

"What elephant? I'm pregnant! By my husband. That's great news! Well, for me, it is." She picked up a piece of cucumber and dunked it in her mouth. "Now, I just need to set the doctor's appointment. I took four pregnancy tests, so I'm pretty sure it's accurate."

"Are you sure, sure?" I flipped through the newspaper that'd been sitting on the counter. "You should maybe get checked before you get your hopes and everyone else's up, Dah."

"Seriously, Cameron? I know my body," she argued, fluffing her shoulder-length, platinum-blonde hair.

"I'm just saying. Nothing's positive yet."

The constant arguing had become the biggest obstacle in our marriage. Camisha brought me so much more peace than Dahlia ever could, but she also wasn't bringing in any paper. Dahlia was, which is why I'd chosen to stay married to her, even though I knew I was madly in love with someone else. When I first met Camisha Janae Atkins, I was just a horny hunk who wasn't getting any good sex at home, so I sought to get it elsewhere. She was a fantasy that I needed to be fulfilled. I'd always dreamed of being intimate with a larger woman, and she fed my longtime fetish. Ever since I'd met her on Aisle 6 in Piggly Wiggly, I'd been on her like a magnet to metal. I was supposed to be doing my job, restocking the cokes, but I was so taken by her that I could barely do that. Being that she was a decade younger than me, I was turned on by the idea of being her sugar daddy, which is why I basically took care of her. I cared for her monetarily, and she cared for me sexually. It was an exchange. I was fine with that arrangement, at first, but in the process, I caught myself up. I let my emotions get the best of me.

I made promises I couldn't keep. Like divorcing my wife. Dahlia and I may have been going through some things, but we both knew that separating wasn't an option.

"Those damn sticks in there all said positive. So, what are you *really* saying?" she yelled, forgetting that our children were upstairs. "Don't upset me."

"What's the attitude for?" I looked up from the sales ad, subsequently putting it down and heading to the refrigerator for a cold beer. "We just spoke on the phone yesterday morning, and you were telling me how happy you'd be to get home to me. So, what's wrong?"

"You really want to know what's wrong, Cameron? Hmph? Do you really want to know?" By this time, she'd gone to the sink, turned on the faucet, and began washing and prepping the lettuce.

"We've always talked about the importance of communication, so tell me!"

"I read that positive pregnancy test and instantly

gained a natural high. Until I realized that I'm the only one carrying the financial weight and have been for months," Dahlia complained. "I'm tired of being the only one who cares enough to make sure that we're good!"

I popped the top off of the Budweiser and said, "I've been trying, Dahlia! You know that I have! I just came from an interview last week!"

Here she goes, again, complaining about me being unemployed. It was almost as if Dahlia thought that I liked being without a job and letting her foot all of the bills.

"Well, you're damn sure not trying hard enough," she shouted, snapping her eyebrows together. "Everything I make goes into this household. I miss when you were able to pull your own weight and when you were able to pick up the tab. You know, when you could actually spoil me!"

"We barely go out for me to even spoil you, Dahlia. You're always busy, remember?" I countered, slowly spinning from side to side on the swivel bar stool. "Why didn't you just stay at your mom's house? Since you act like you really don't want to be here anyway."

"This is my goddamn house, too, Cameron!" Dahlia raised her squeaky, mouse-like voice, her blue eyes growing with every word that flew from her thin, parted lips. "And you know why? Because I'd rather eat at home than suffer the embarrassment of the waiter slapping the check down in front of me. Me! The woman. The woman who thought she'd married a real man."

"So, the amount of income I bring in determines my worth as a man now?" I sized her up, taking a swig of my beverage. "That's a new one."

When Dahlia and I first tied the knot ten years ago, I'd just gotten on at Coca-Cola, and she was pregnant with our daughter, Kennedy. We'd been dating for seven years and engaged for two of those, so it made sense to finally jump the broom. I'd known this girl since my senior year in high school; she was my heart… my everything. And vice versa. I wasn't perfect, but I was perfect for her. She saw past the guy from the projects, with baggy clothes and a beat-up grill. She helped me get my shit together and straightened me up whenever I tried to go off track. Up until we were married, we stayed in the basement of her grandparents' home. Ain't that some shit? While she would be in school getting her Business degree, her grandfather would pay me to help him with yard work and anything else that needed to be done around the house.

Her grandparents prided her on her choice to go to college and make something of herself. God rest their souls. Honestly, if it wasn't for them and her, I wouldn't be the man I am today. Dahlia saw my potential, made me want to be somebody influential. She'd come from the All-American family. Whereas I was catching the bus in school, her parents were taking her to cop a fresh-off-the-lot ride. We were different, but through our different dynamics, we made the ultimate blend. With her, by my side, I became a better man, a better husband, and a better father. I knew from the moment I laid eyes on her that she was the good woman I'd mistaken the bad bitches for. Because of that, I wanted to give her the world because I knew that she was special, and she deserved it.

Then came the children and the careers. Dahlia had always loved nice things and fancy shit. So, when it came down to her dream of being an interior designer, I supported her. Her very first client was a person at my job. The fellow workers at the Coca-Cola plant had heard me bragging about my wife's décor skills and wanted to see if her work matched the hype. It did, and from there, her clientele grew tremendously. Dahlia Dargan is the most notable interior designer in Anniston, Alabama, but her name rings bells all over the south. At the beginning of her career, she was traveling so much that she barely had any personal belongings at home; they were all on the road with her. Before the kids came of school age, they stayed with nannies and relatives while Dahlia and I hustled our asses off to provide the life that we always wanted our children to have. Up until a few months ago, we'd exceeded at doing so. Coca-Cola laid off a batch of employees, and I just so happened to be one of them. It was a real adjustment having to be at home every day, on my ass. I thought that was a thing of the past for me. I guess I was wrong. It made me feel like nothing, all over again. Fuck a housewife; I had turned into a househusband. Getting the kids ready for school, cooking, putting them to bed. It all drew Dahlia and me further and further apart from each other. As if we weren't already divided.

Somewhere along the way, we forgot about us. Well, Dahlia forgot about me. I never forgot about her... intentionally. Even with my job, I still tried to keep things spicy between us, but she stopped feeling the heat, and the flame eventually died. So, I sparked a new one with someone else, while being married, and it turned into a full-blown fire. A fire that I have yet to put out, and I wasn't so sure if I wanted to.

Dahlia's parents predicted that our relationship wouldn't last, and we should've listened. They were never too fond of their white daughter dating a Black man, and they told us to our faces that we would never work out. She wanted to prove them wrong, and us breaking up would only prove them right. When they saw that we were getting serious, they kicked Dahlia out, and that's how she ended up at her grandparents'. Me, on the other hand, didn't have that to worry about. My mother died an hour after giving birth to me. My father, an African man she'd met on a military base, hadn't been seen or heard from since he'd knocked her up with me, during a one-night stand. So, I was raised by my aunt, my mother's sister, Geraldine Dargan. I was her baby boy; in her eyes, I was her son, the one she'd always wanted but was never able to have, biologically. I remember when I first introduced her to Dahlia, she loved her. Now, she couldn't stand her. Dahlia had gotten a little fortune and a little fame, and it all rushed to her head. Aunt Geraldine was as humble as they come, and she was quick to pull Dahlia off of her high-horse. Dahlia didn't like that, and my wife being the outspoken person she is, she told her. Over dinner, in my aunt's dining room.

    Aunt Geraldine pulled a knife on Dahlia for trying to disrespect her in her "shack," as Dahlia called it, and she's been prohibited from seeing my children or me since then. But the choice wasn't made by me. It was made by Dahlia, who'd already discussed that she wanted nothing more to do with Aunt G and didn't want me to have anything to do with her either. To keep the peace, I agreed not to. We'd talk over the phone when Dahlia wasn't around, but that was about it.

SIDE CHICKS CATCH FEELINGS TOO

She always tells me how controlling Dahlia is and that I need to have my own voice for once. A part of it was true, but Aunt G didn't know the Dahlia who I knew and loved. The Dahlia who had my back, through any weather. We were just having marital problems. Problems that a therapy session could probably fix if we really wanted to. But were they that bad? I don't know. I didn't realize that I wasn't in love with Dahlia anymore until I'd fallen in love with someone else. And I hated myself for that. I hated myself for allowing it to go this far, to get this deep. I just couldn't help myself.

I loved Camisha. I took care of her when I had money and even now when I don't, I still do. I'd go in the joint account that Dahlia and I shared and get hundreds of dollars for Camisha. Her rent, I still paid it. Her car note, I still paid it. I had her thinking that it was still coming straight out of my pocket. The whole time, it was coming out of my wife's purse. Whenever Dahlia asked me where the money was going, I told her that I was gambling it away at poker night with the fellas. That caused havoc in our marriage, too, but I'd rather feed her a lie than to tell her the cold-hearted truth. The truth that her husband was pussy-whipped and driven insane by a tenderoni. She'd tried to get me to go get some help for my so-called "addiction," but I didn't need help with that. The only addiction I had was to Camisha, and that shit doesn't even seem curable. But, after her finding out that I'd gotten Dahlia pregnant, it'd have to be. I knew that she wanted nothing else to do with me. She hadn't called or texted. This wasn't like her. I was for certain that I'd lost her this time.

Dahlia and I continued our argument in the kitchen. She kept throwing jabs at me about how I wasn't bringing anything to the table, and how she could eat alone. She eventually grew tired of talking to a brick wall, finished up dinner, and called the kids down to eat. She'd made a humongous taco salad. My favorite. Her pale skin didn't define her culinary skills. I enjoyed everything she cooked. Well, when she had time to cook it.

The tension at the dining-room table was so thick that you could chop it up in blocks. Dahlia didn't say anything to me; I didn't say anything to her. The kids talked amongst each other, giggling and carrying on until they couldn't giggle or carry on any longer. When done, I got up, dropped my plate into the dishwasher, grabbed another cold Budweiser from the refrigerator and chugged it, before I prepared to leave. She sent the children upstairs to get their backpacks so that they could pull out their homework. Normally, I'd stay and help, but I needed time to get my head together. Dahlia had pissed me off to the point of no return. Lately, nothing I did was ever enough. It wasn't my fault that

SIDE CHICKS CATCH FEELINGS TOO

I'd gotten laid off and had a hard time finding something else. At least I was trying. But, to her, that didn't seem to mean anything. Instead, she wanted to kick me while I was down, which was only pushing me further into the arms of someone else.

Not even an hour later, I was knocking on Camisha's door, hoping and praying that she would let me in. I hadn't called or texted her because I knew that she, more than likely, wouldn't respond to me. Whenever we did argue, which was rare, she was the type to shut down and let me mend things... after she'd sent me three long paragraphs about how she felt. I wasn't so sure if this could even be mended this time, though.

The rain poured something awful as I waited for her to answer the door. Raindrops were intensely hitting the pavement, the clouds began to darken, and lightning started to cut through the sky. With my hands tucked in my blue slacks, nervousness began to set in. The taste of beer was still in my mouth, so I was sure that my breath smelled of it too. I searched around my pocket and grabbed the box of Tic Tacs before popping a few in my mouth. I never showed up unannounced. I probably looked like a fool... just as much as I felt like a fool. Who was I to expect her to welcome me with open arms, especially after what she'd just discovered? Dahlia was pregnant, and there was nothing that I could do about it. There was no excuse that I could give that would make sense. Talking Dahlia into getting an abortion wouldn't work, so this was just something that I'd have to accept. It wouldn't be easy, but I'd made my own bed hard, so I would have to make it soft.

"What is it, Cameron?" Camisha asked, cracking the door just enough for half of her face to be shown. "Why are you here? The damage is done, so I don't give a damn about what you came over here to say."

"Just hear me out, Misha. Please," I begged, raising my shirt to wipe the rain from my face. "We could get through this."

"Get through this?" She laughed, taking me as a joke. "Are you hearing yourself right now, Cameron? You sound like a fucking dumb ass."

"Camisha, I really didn't mean for her to get pregnant," I explained, nervously rubbing my hands together. "It just happened."

"Well, the chances of that happening are even higher when you fuck someone without a condom," she spat sarcastically, preparing to shut the door in my face before I caught it. "Leave me the fuck alone!"

"No, I'm not leaving you alone, Misha," I seriously said. "We're going to figure this shit out. Like we did the last time."

"You didn't get her pregnant, Cameron. That's the difference." She inched the door open a little further, now revealing her whole face. That pretty-ass, mocha-painted face I'd always loved. The one with the deep-ass dimples, the small patch of freckles underneath each of those dreamy, brown eyes, and the cute double chin that I often enjoyed planting sloppy kisses on. Camisha was beautiful. She was short, with a nice grade of jet-black hair. I was so glad that she'd taken those damn braids, or whatever the hell they were, out of her hair so that I could play in her mane. Seeing her in her natural state accentuated her beauty, to me. So beautiful and so vivacious. Curves wide enough to throw any man off course, breasts large enough to supply milk for us all, feet pretty enough to make your mouth water at the sight of them, lips juicy enough to wrap around the biggest... hmm.

But, at this moment, she was acting so ugly toward me.

Leslie McDaniels. She's who I was talking about when I said we'd 'figure this out like we did the last time.' Leslie was my former co-worker who I'd had a brief affair with a few years back. She was attractive, but with that attraction came craziness. She'd vent to me about how she'd been having dreams of killing her ex-husband for marrying her sister, and how she'd even been Googling how to do so. I sort of became her shoulder to lean on, which was the biggest mistake I could've ever made.

Hey, blame temptation; not me. Even the most unbothered fish will eventually catch the bait if it's being thrown in its face constantly. That's what happened to me. I wasn't interested in Leslie like that, but she was interested in me. She was so interested that she seduced me, and idiotically, I fell for it. We fooled around a couple of times... until I had to file a restraining order. She was stalking me. One night, I'd fallen asleep in her bed, and she decided to snap a photo of me. To take it even further, she'd gotten Camisha's number out of my phone, and assuming that she was my wife, she sent her the picture.

Camisha was hurt. Knowing that she had basically been competing against Dahlia was already too much, but knowing that it was someone else, too? Oh, she was furiously heartbroken. But we eventually overcame it, together. I said that I would never do that to her again, but now look. Now, just fucking look. It'd been seven, long years with Camisha. Seven, long years that I wasn't just willing to throw away at the drop of a dime. I wasn't going to let her walk away from me like this. I couldn't.

"Let's just let that go." I leaned forward. "Alright?"

"You brought it up! You need to go, Cameron." She

turned to walk away before I pulled her into me. "Get off of me!"

"I'm not going anywhere!" I refused, letting her out of my embrace. "Can I come in? It's storming!"

She sighed deeply, placing her right hand on top of her forehead. She then stepped away from the door to let me inside. Inside of the apartment that I paid for, that I held the rights to, that I should've been able to come up in whenever I damn well pleased.

I shut the door behind me, going over to the leather-wrapped loveseat. I propped my arms on the back of it and crossed my legs, waiting for her to join me. She'd done a lot more decorating since my last visit, which was two months ago. Most of our fucking happened at my home, so I rarely ever came over to Camisha's, unless Dahlia and the kids were around. I'd usually meet her to give her the money for rent and other bills in Save A Lot's parking lot. I honestly missed this little place, though. I missed the peace that came with not having to sneak around, not having to be on pins and needles, or stay on my P's and Q's. I could just be me, Cam. Cam Dargie or Cam Money, as Camisha and I would joke around and say. Without the judgment or constant reminders that I didn't have shit from Dahlia.

Camisha walked to the kitchen, her fat rump jiggling with every step that she took. *Jesus.* Just being around this fine-ass woman made my dick as hard as a rock. That pink-and-green floral sundress that she had on didn't make it any better. She took a paper towel from its roll, sprayed some all-purpose Lysol cleaner on it and washed the countertops. Her arms moved in a circular motion, along with the towel and her hand. I couldn't help but think about how her succulent ass would clap against me, as each of my hands was fixed tightly around her cinnamon-coated love handles. To me, it was so fucking sexy how the rest of her body was a shade lighter than her face. And I loved that big, black-ass birthmark that sat between her voluptuous-ass, luscious thighs like a burnt spot on buttered, toasted bread. Just thinking about it had me hungry for more.

A lot had gone down in that kitchen. I'd eaten Camisha for breakfast, lunch, dinner, and hell, even a late-night snack. Yep, right on the tile flooring that she stood on at this very moment. Those were the days. She hadn't too long moved into this apartment, and things were like peaches and cream between us. Sometimes, we'd be so loud and so rough that we'd get complaints from the neighbors. Those were some good, fun times. We didn't have a care in the world; we only cared about each other. Back then we genuinely enjoyed each other's company. If I let Camisha get away now, all of that would be gone down the drain. I'd made my best memories with this woman. Memories that I'd cherish forever and wanted to keep making.

"Can I get you some tea or water?" she offered, as I continued looking around the apartment, reminiscing.

She had an obsession with elephants. Anything elephant-printed or sculpted, she wanted it.

"Yeah, water. Cold, please," I requested, watching her get a glass from the Cherrywood cabinet above the Maytag microwave. Her small height called for her to jump in order to be able to reach it, and the sight of that was quite amusing. "So, are we going to talk about this?"

She fumbled with the built-in ice maker on her refrigerator. The one that I'd paid off for her. We'd both gone furniture shopping at Aaron's and picked it out. I never understood women's hype about fancy appliances, especially when they all served the same purpose and would get used the same way. But what Camisha wanted, she always got. Maybe it was those puppy-dog eyes, or maybe it was the way she'd mouth, "Pleaaasseeee, Daddy?!" Oh, yeah, that seemed to do the trick every time.

"I already told you..."

"Told me what?" I kissed my teeth, adjusting the silver class ring on my manicured pinky finger.

"There's nothing to discuss. You got that bitch pregnant," Camisha said, sitting the misty glass down atop the light-brown coaster on the coffee table in front of me. The color of the table matched the cabinets. Coordination, that was her thing, too. I remembered every detail about this woman, even the little ones.

"So, where do we go from here?" I obtained the cup from the coaster and traced the rim of it. "What's next?"

"Nothing's next. This is just another excuse for you to hold off the divorce," she claimed, her eyes still red and puffy. I could tell that she'd been crying. For me, she was weak, which was something that I admired about her. She wasn't afraid of vulnerability. Dahlia was always so strong and guarded. She'd never, ever give up her control to let me lead like a man is supposed to lead. She hadn't since I'd been married to her. "You probably did this shit on purpose!"

"On purpose? Is that really what you think?"

"Why else would you do it then?" she pressed, taking a seat on the long couch and staring at me. She simultaneously had this look of pain and anger etched on her face. This was worse than when she'd found out about Leslie. I'd never felt this type of energy from Camisha, and I wanted it to stop.

"It was a mistake!"

Camisha fell silent. Awkwardness filled the gloomy-like room. No lights were on, no TV—nothing. I could feel the sadness… the depression. Even the blinds were closed. Not that there was any sunlight to beam in, but still. By the way the dimness took over the space, one would think it was nighttime. She buried her head into her hands and let out a deep sob.

"A mistake?! Is that all you have to say?!" Snot ran out of her nostrils as she lifted her head back up and leered my way. "It wasn't a fucking mistake."

"I can fix this, Misha. I can fix it!" I promised, shaking the ice around in my water before taking a drink of it. "I'll take care of my kids, but I'll also tell Dahlia what it is."

"Fix it? Okay, well, tell her to get a damn abortion then! How about that?" she demanded. "Dahlia already knows what it is between you and me! But she doesn't care, Cameron! Can't you see that?"

"What? Have you told her?" I rose up, gnawing on the cube of ice with my back teeth. "Camisha, did you?!"

"No!" she answered, giving me a sense of relief. "I just feel like she knows about us, Cameron. Why do you think she's always conveniently gone on the weekends? She's okay with letting you have your fun on the side, as long as she has a piece of you."

"You sound foolish. She doesn't know about us, and I would like to keep it that way," I said. "And no, she won't agree to an abortion! What kind of father would that make me, to even suggest some shit like that?"

"There's no us unless you get rid of her, and I know that's not going to happen."

"She'll always be in my life because of the kids, Misha," I admitted. "Kennedy and Jaxon need their parents."

"And they can still have y'all, but y'all don't have to be together!"

"Okay, I'll break things off with her," I hesitantly said. As easy as I was making it sound, it wouldn't be. "But have you ever sat to think about how this would impact my babies?"

I couldn't tell Camisha that if I ended things with Dahlia, she wouldn't have a place to stay, and the cash flow would stop. So, I used my kids as a pawn.

"Do it. Or should I?" Camisha threatened.

"No, keep your mouth shut or I'm reneging on our agreement."

"What agreement?" She acted cluelessly.

"This..." I whirled my index finger up in the air. "Your stuff will be on the side of the road, and you won't have a pot to piss in. Don't play with me, Misha. I love you, and I really don't want to have to go that route."

"Oh, really? That's what we're doing now?" She

drew her chin into her neck. "What's the difference in me telling her and you telling her? What's me telling her going to hurt?"

"Just don't. I know Dahlia, and I know how to work through the kinks. You coming to her will only make things worse."

"You can't tell me what to do, Cameron!" she yelled. "Get rid of her, or I'll do it myself."

"You won't do shit." I chuckled. "Just relax. Let's approach this like adults."

"Relax? Approach this like adults?"

"You heard what I said."

"I heard exactly what you said!" She folded her arms in dismay and scooted to the edge of the sofa. "It's either me or her. I can't do this any longer!"

Camisha came into this knowing that I was married. I may have not been one hundred percent truthful about where Dahlia and I stood, but she was still my wife. How could Camisha expect me not to fuck on Dahlia once in a blue moon? I'm a man; I have needs. When Camisha isn't fulfilling them, that's what Dahlia is for. Vice versa. Every time I want to have sex, I'm supposed to get out of bed and go hunt her down? It was these unrealistic ways of thinking that always reminded me of her age.

"It's not about you or her. It's about Kennedy, Jaxon,

and my unborn one."

"So, you're choosing to be unhappy because of the kids? They don't even know what the fuck is going on!" She raised her voice again. I shushed her, putting my finger to my lip.

"It's complicated," I huffed. "Camisha, just bear with me, please!"

"I've been bearing with you long enough!" she exclaimed. "Let's just..."

"Just what?" I proceeded to listen.

"Eliminate her ourselves." Her tune changed as if a lightbulb had gone off in her head.

"Eliminate her? What do you mean?" I grew alarmed.

A devilish grin crept across Camisha's face. I had an idea of what she was about to say, but I don't think I wanted to believe that such a thing could be coming from her mouth.

"Kill her. Kill her so we can be happy, without any of the interruptions," she revealed matter-of-factly.

"The fuck?! Killing her would mean killing my child! I can't do that! I-I-I can't take my kids' mother away from them! I can't go to jail! What the hell are you saying right now?!" I exclaimed, as I sat my water down and leaped to my feet.

"Do you love me as much as you say you do,

Cameron?" Camisha interrogated, purring in her tone.

I stayed quiet, still trying to take in what she'd just suggested.

"Answer me! Do you love me?" she continued on.

"Y-Y-Yes!" I stuttered. "But I don't love you more than my children."

"And I never tried to get you to do so!" she yelled. "But can't you see?"

"Can't I see what?"

"Dahlia is causing a rift between us!" She slapped her chest, highlighting the infinity tattoo on her exposed upper body, with the letter 'C' underneath it. "I don't want to lose you, but I can't stand by you if she's bringing another one of your children in this world!"

My heart was pounding and sweat began to crowd my forehead.

"Camisha, we can't do that," I objected. "Do you know what type of traction her murder would bring? In this city? There's no way we would ever get out of that. The cops would find out."

My faint knees brought me back onto the couch, pondering and panting. Why was I even entertaining this idea? Is this really coming from Camisha? I had to take a minute and analyze things. A part of me wanted to go through with this plan, while a part of me was disgusted at the mere thought of it. This was my wife, the woman I'd taken vows before God with. The woman I produced two of the best little people that have ever happened to me. How could I consider doing that to her? To my kids? What kind of man—matter of fact, human being—would that make me? I mean, getting rid of Dahlia would cure the headache that she brought me. And it would save me the guilt of having to break the news to her about my double life. It would also allow me to live happily ever after with Camisha. But was it worth it?

"Or would they?" She came over to me and straddled my lap, gazing into my eyes. "She's been messing up what we have for far too long."

"You're right, but—"

Camisha interjected, shutting me up with a kiss.

She then pulled the straps to her dress from her shoulder and brought her boobs up out of her bra and into my mouth.

"Hmmmm," she moaned as I sucked and bit gently on each one. "Ooooh, shit."

As soon as I dropped her left titty out of my grip, she jumped from my lap and to her knees, unbuckling my pants. I couldn't fight it, not even if I wanted to. She plunged my penis into her jaws, tickling my balls with her fingertips. The feeling of her tongue ring colliding with the skin on my Johnson sent me into ecstasy, making my eyes roll to the back of my head. Thrusting myself down her throat, precum began oozing out of my dick. She was coughing, spitting, and then slurping back up the same saliva that'd just left her mouth.

"You like that, Daddy?" she provocatively slurred, raunchily peering up at me.

"Fuck! I do, Misha! I do!" I grunted, running my fingers through her hair.

She'd given me head for about a good ten minutes before I nutted everywhere, and even then, she wouldn't stop until I had to push her off of me.

"Now, has your mind changed?" she inquired, getting up from the floor and dabbing the corners of her mouth.

"I have to go," I stated.

Dammit, Camisha.

What have you done to me?

CHAPTER FOUR

CAMISHA "MISHA" ATKINS

Sucking Cameron's dick wasn't on the agenda when he came over here the other day, but he just looked so damn good that I couldn't resist. And as much as I tried to tell myself that I didn't want him anymore, or I didn't have any hopes of repairing our union, I still did. It was stupid of me to think that these feelings would disappear overnight, even though I was wishing that they would. Once I'd gotten him off, he was out of the door faster than I could wave goodbye, and I was left with a wet pussy and a sore throat. *Men*. Cameron had done the most disrespectful thing that could ever be done to a woman: he ghosted before he could return the oral favor. I actually hadn't heard anything from him since, and surprisingly, I hadn't tried to reach out to him either. I was confused. I was filled with so many mixed emotions. I hated how much I still loved him.

For seven years, Cameron had been a part of my everyday life. This was someone who I envisioned building a family and spending forever with. I thought that sleeping on it would make this hurt subside, but it only strengthened. I was still angry and it'd damn near been a week since I found out that Dahlia was pregnant. I needed closure. Him showing up to my place had given me a sense of closure, but it didn't give me the closure that I needed. After he'd failed to call or text last week, following my departure from his home, I was convinced that I'd hear nothing more from him. I guess I was wrong. When he knocked on my door the very next day, that let me know that I wasn't the only one who still cared and wanted this. And, suddenly, I didn't feel so bad for still caring and still wanting it anymore because I wasn't alone. But I couldn't go back to him under the same conditions; the circumstances would have to change. Dahlia would have to go, for good. At this point, it was fuck her.

Fuck her for ruining the picture-perfect lifestyle that I had set in stone for Cameron and I. Fuck her for being everything that I wanted to be to Cameron. *His everything.* He was supposed to divorce her, and we were supposed to get married, go for full custody of Kennedy and Jaxon, then have them another brother or sister. That was what Cameron and I talked about. But then he goes and does this? He gets her pregnant and ruins everything. I blame Cameron, but I blame Dahlia more.

I blame her for still holding on to a man who clearly wanted to let her go. I blame her for using those kids as a way to keep him somewhere he didn't want to be kept.

Cameron has always been an exceptional father, which was the main reason why I wanted to experience that dimension of him. I wanted to have his babies, and give my children a childhood similar to the one that I had—minus the overbearing husband of the household and wife with the do-girl mentality. I wanted to create my own family, my own way. Dahlia having another kid would only delay that for me. So, yeah, removing her from the equation was vital. I loved Cameron, and I was aware that ending our relationship wasn't something I was quite emotionally ready for yet.

But I needed him on board. I needed him to help me save us if this is what he really and truly wanted. He could've shitted a load of bricks when I brought up the idea of murdering Dahlia during his short stay. I didn't see a problem with getting rid of her, considering how unsatisfied he was in their marriage. At least, that's the bullshit he's been telling me. I thought that giving him some neck would leave him no choice but to agree, but he punked out. Her being gone would only make our lives better, happier. Well, for me, it would. I'd finally have the man of my dreams... all to myself. I wouldn't have to continue settling for a fraction of him.

The noisy buzz from my phone sounding off on the kitchen counter awakened me from my daze. It could've been

SIDE CHICKS CATCH FEELINGS TOO

Cameron, but I didn't feel like moving from my comfortable position on the hot-pink, plush throw rug. Besides, his reaction to what I'd suggested rubbed me the wrong way. He was frightened, and I could see it. Why the fuck should he even care if that bitch is dead or alive? Now, he was pissing me the fuck off, again. Yeah, he wants to think about the kids, but what about him? What about me? After all, I have been the most important woman in his life for damn near a decade. Though he's been there for me financially, emotionally, I've been the glue holding Cameron together. For the past few months, he's been depressed about some shit that he has yet to tell me about, and who did he call during the night to relieve that stress? Me. He'd literally get out of his own bed, with his wife, and go into the guest bedroom to have phone sex on FaceTime with me. There were also some times that he'd even come over here.

I finally checked my Samsung Galaxy S9 and saw that I had a new message on Facebook Messenger. It was Mimi, asking if I wanted to meet somewhere for lunch. That was dumb, considering that she had my number, but I still replied. I agreed to meet at a nearby Mexican restaurant, which was only a mile or two up the road from where I lived. It was three o'clock in the afternoon, and I hadn't been awake for too long, so I told her to give me an hour. A bitch had to get dressed and get my mind right. It was all over the place, particularly on if I could talk Cameron into my scheme of scraping Dahlia off of his nuts and getting her out of the way permanently. It may take some time, but I was confident that I could get him to break. There was almost nothing I couldn't get Cameron to do. I was his queen. Unlike Dahlia.

Dahlia may have looked like a bitch, talked like a bitch, but she wasn't as bold as she portrayed herself to be. She was just bitter. Bitter that, no matter how many dark hair dyes or chocolate penises she partook in, she could never be as Black as the woman who was capable of taking her Black man away from her. I've known women like her throughout my whole life. The color of their skin often makes them feel superior as if they have gold between their legs and up the cracks of their asses. If they can hold the key to a Black man's heart, they feel like they're holding the key to life. In Dahlia's case, she wasn't holding either. She didn't have Cameron's heart; I did. And soon enough, I'd have her life, too.

 It was fifteen minutes or so after four when I arrived at my favorite Mexican spot.

 I pulled into a parking space near the door. I was delighted that the lunch crowd at Los Arcos had come and gone, and there were only a few vehicles outside. Those could've very well belonged to the workers. The weather had cleared, and the sun was beginning to peek out again. I was actually glad that it'd been raining a lot lately because this July heat was no joke, and we needed something to cool it down. This was one time that I didn't worry about burning gas; the air conditioner in my Malibu never went off. I couldn't imagine riding around without it. On days like this, I thanked God for it. Just as I thought, Mimi wasn't here yet. She could never be on time for anything. Hell, I was almost positive that she wouldn't even be on time for her own funeral, and you know that's sad.

While I waited for Mimi to pull up, I let the visor down and applied a coat of my Jelly Pop Juicy Gloss by e.l.f. Cosmetics, in the shade Watermelon Pop. It was too hot for makeup, and I wasn't meeting anyone who required me to put on any. So, a good gloss always did the trick. I just threw on an oversized, white Gadsden State Community College t-shirt, along with a pair of black leggings, and called it a day. I was comfortable, and that's all that mattered. No sooner than I logged into my PayPal account to check my balance, I heard someone blowing their horn repeatedly as they drove up behind me. It was Mimi, being her usual, boisterous self. What would I do without people like her in my life?

I killed the engine and got out of the car. She did the same, rushing over to give me a hug. You'd think it'd been one year instead of one week since we'd last seen each other.

"Where are Maddy and Asia?" I asked, seeing that she was alone.

"They're with my mom," she answered, as she pulled her blue jean shorts out of her inner thighs. "Girl, it's Saturday. I needed some me time."

"I feel that," I said, stepping up onto the sidewalk that led to the building. We both walked into the restaurant and were seated by the hostess.

"What's going on with you? How are you feeling today?" Mimi questioned, sitting her purse down in the chair next to her before taking a look at the menu that the hostess had just placed in front of us.

I took a seat across from her, bringing myself closer to the table. "To tell you the truth, I don't know what I'm feeling."

"You should be fed the fuck up." Mimi surveyed the Western-designed eatery, lapping both arms on top of each other on the ceramic surface.

That was easy for someone like Miana Walker to say. At twenty-six years old, my best friend's list of love and relationships was longer than a five-page essay. Some would say and think that it was probably because she was one of the biggest whores in Calhoun County, which wasn't true, while I would say that it was simply because she was gorgeous.

Absolutely gorgeous. Beyond Jeremy, her boo thang, she had a line of other men waiting to be chosen. So, the saying, "Men are like buses. One comes every fifteen minutes," had been deemed true in her case. For me, the fat girl, it hadn't always.

My sister from another mister's beautifully-tanned skin often had people thinking that she was from the islands. She was 5'6", with curly, dark-brown hair that came to her shoulders. Even though she rarely ever wore it out. She enjoyed skipping the hassle of maintaining her own and slapping on a wig. I couldn't be mad at that. The tiny gaps between her teeth and underbite didn't take away from the fact that her face was perfection; acne-free and proportioned just right. Her eyebrows were thick but naturally-arched. Her nose was Hollywood-ready. Her lips were the shape of a supermodel's. After having two kids, her once slim frame had sprouted out in all the right areas. She was what all the guys wanted. Tyson definitely missed out and messed up.

"You're right; I should be," I agreed, placing my keys and my Michael Kors wristlet on the far end of the table, near the napkin holder and salt-and-pepper shakers. "But I kind of feel like I'm not. I feel like there's more to him and me. You know? I've put too much into this to let it all go."

"You do know how stupid you sound, right?" Mimi sarcastically questioned.

"Hello, I'm your waitress, Catalina," the burgundy-haired server—with oval-shaped eyes and Spanish features—introduced herself. She had to be a little person; she was shorter than me, and I was pretty short. "What could I start you guys off to drink with?"

"Just water with lemon for me," I told her. "Light on the ice, please."

She nodded her head.

"I guess I won't drink today, since I'm driving." Mimi laughed. "I'll take a sprite."

"Okay, I'll be back with those drinks in just a second," the waitress informed us before whipping out her notepad. "Do you guys need a minute to order, or do you know what you want?"

I scanned the place, spotting the table that Cameron and I usually sat at, in the back. Any other day, I'd be here with him, sharing margaritas and talking about how good we'd made each other feel the night before. But Mimi would just have to do.

"Hmmm, I think I'll go with what I always get. The fiesta fajita bowl," I ordered, scratching the side of my face. "Mimi, what about you?"

"Is that good? What does it come with?" she asked, studying the menu. "I want something that's really cheesy."

"Girl, it's really good and cheesy. Comes with rice, onions, peppers, shrimp, chicken, steak—everything!"

"Yes, it's delicious," Catalina chimed in, her accent thick in her speech. "You won't regret trying it."

"Well, y'all better be right, or one of you will be responsible for paying for my meal," Mimi joked. "I'll get that."

We all let out a laugh.

"Coming right up," Catalina said, before walking away.

Once she was out of sight, I proceeded on with the conversation Mimi and I was having.

"Back to what we were talking about. How am I the one who looks stupid?"

"Camisha, that man is married. Been married since y'all first started messing around. If he hasn't gotten rid of his wife by now, he won't ever," Mimi spoke her piece. "I think you should move on."

"Move on? Let's be realistic, Mimi. I just found out this shit yesterday. Moving on takes time."

"I know that. Trust me, I know that better than anybody. But you aren't even trying to make the first step."

Mimi and I became friends in the ninth grade, and she hadn't changed since. She would tell me the truth, whether I liked it or not, whether it hurt or healed me. That was one of the things I loved and hated about her ass. She always told me something that I didn't want to hear, but it would end up being what I needed to hear. Right now, I didn't want to hear that I should give up on Cameron and what we had. I just didn't. I wasn't giving up shit. Dahlia was. Mark my words. I couldn't tell Mimi that, though. I didn't need her two cents on my decision to take Dahlia out. She'd only try to talk me out of doing it when I knew that this was something that had to be done. How it would be done was the one thing to figure out, though.

"The first step? What would be the first step, Mimi?" I acted interested in what it was that she was about to say, knowing damn well that I wasn't and was still going to do whatever the fuck I wanted to do. "What do you suggest? Since you have all the answers."

"Hey, pipe down, bitch. I'm not the one you should be mad at." She threw her hands up in surrender. "I'm just saying; in order to heal, you must remove what is hurting you."

Catalina returned with our drinks, a basket of tortilla chips, and a bowl of salsa. "Your food should be up in a while. Let me know if you need anything."

"Thank you," I said shakily. "I love him, Mimi. I love him so much."

"Well, love him enough to let him go," she uttered, sipping some of her soda. "You remember how you used to complain to me about your mother relying too much on your father?"

"Yeah, but what does this have to do with that?" A look of confusion shot across my face.

"Because you're doing the same exact thing. You're too dependent on Cameron," Mimi expressed. "Monetarily and emotionally. You just don't see it."

"Are you serious?"

"I'm so serious, Mish," she replied, drenching her chip in the sauce. "You can't breathe without him. That isn't healthy."

"Healthy? So, now, I'm a mental patient?" I sneered. "You've got to be fucking kidding me. Don't act like your shit don't stink."

"I never said it didn't! Stop getting so defensive, girl," she talked through a covered mouth as she ate.

"I'm not getting defensive." Tears sat at my lower lash line. "But what you're not about to do is sit up here and act like I'm crazy for loving a man who has given me every reason to love him. I can't help what I feel."

"So, him having another baby with his wife didn't change anything?"

"Of course, it did. But if he breaks it off with Dahlia

completely and focuses on me, maybe we could start fresh," I said feeling a bit hopeful.

"Must be the spices in the salsa that are messing with my allergies." She turned her head away from the table and sneezed into her forearm. "That baby still isn't going to go away, even if Dahlia does. You're setting yourself up for even more heartbreak, but okay, you do you, and I'll do me."

"And Jeremy," I ragged, trying to lighten the mood and slickly change the subject.

"Yes, bitch. I'ma do every inch of Jeremy's fine ass." She stuck her tongue out of her mouth.

"Moving on from all of my drama, how are you and J?" I pried, getting the spotlight off of me.

"We're good, but the other night, we weren't."

"Two fiesta fajita bowls," our waitress came whirling over to us with the food, pulling us away from our ongoing chatter.

"Could I have some extra onions?" Mimi asked, as our plates were being sat down on our table. She then reached for her phone from her bosom, opened the camera, and took a picture of her entrée.

"Sure, coming right up," Catalina responded. "Could I get you some more water, ma'am?"

"Yes, please," I said, dangling my half-empty cup. I

must've been thirsty.

She grabbed my cup and took it to the back with her.

"Now, what happened between you and J?" I resumed with Mimi.

For the remainder of our lunch, Mimi released her frustration about Jeremy's inability to give her sex fifty times a day. She claimed that he'd be out with the fellas most of the time, which tired him out by nightfall. Now, don't get me wrong; fucking like wild animals was a must in a relationship, but Mimi had always been the type to create problems that weren't even there. All she literally had to do was sit her pussy on that man's face, and suddenly, he'd wake right the fuck up. Maybe it was due to what I was going through with Cameron or the nagging fly that someone had let in the restaurant door, but I was getting agitated. As soon as I finished my food, I told Mimi that I had another engagement to make it to and hauled ass to my car. She asked where, and I lied about having some Mary Kay party that my aunt had invited me to. I really was just trying to get away so that I could contact Cameron. Thank God she didn't ask to come with me.

"Hello?" I spoke into the receiver once he picked up.

"What is it, Misha?" he answered in a bothered tone. The nerve of this nigga.

"Where are you?"

"Work."

"You don't work on Saturdays, Cameron. Especially not after two," I called him out. "I need to see you."

"See me for what? I'm not up with that about Dahlia," he whispered.

"We don't need to discuss this over the phone," I stopped him. "Meet me near the old bridge behind AutoZone and Anniston Middle School."

"For what?"

"I'll be there in five minutes... waiting for you."

I hung up on him and fired up the Malibu.

"In order to heal, you have to remove what's hurting you," I replayed Mimi's words in my head in again.

She was right. Dahlia was what was hurting me.

CHAPTER FIVE

CAMERON "CAM" DARGAN

"I like the plaid tie better. Makes you look like you belong," Dahlia critiqued, as she sat at her old-time, cream-colored vanity, brushing through her flaxen tresses. "Pair it with the black button-up instead of the blue one."

The smell of TRESemmé hair spray pervaded the air, causing me to cough and sniff a bit. Anytime my wife stepped out of the house, she was always at her best. Dahlia Annabella Casey was a beauty queen; there was no denying that. Her eyes were as blue as the Pacific Ocean, with hair that flowed like the heavy waves within it. Her shape wasn't the fullest, but her personality made up for that. Her teeth were so straight that they'd often get mistaken for veneers, her cheekbones were so high that if seen by actress Cameron Diaz, she'd even get offended. Dahlia kept the sparkles on her clothes and the diamonds on her finger. Glitter, glamour, and gold were the three things every girl needed, in her opinion. Her choice of lipstick was MAC Cosmetics' Ruby Red. But, in comparison, Dahlia Annabella damn sure was no Camisha Janae, or CJ, as I sometimes referred to her as.

"How long will this thing last?" I asked, pacing the floor of the master bedroom of our five-bedroom house.

"Don't want to be out too late. The kids may get restless at Jamie's."

After the phone call I'd just received from Camisha, I didn't know what to think or how to feel. I wanted to see her, but my mind just wouldn't stop repeating what she'd proposed that day at her apartment. The proposal to get rid of the woman I took an oath before God with—my wife, Dahlia. I now looked at Camisha differently, and it scared me because I didn't know whether it was in a good or bad way. Murder Dahlia? Really? If I were to go through with it, how would I explain the death of their mother to Kennedy and Jaxon? I don't even know if I could face them knowing that I was the reason behind their mother's demise. Knowing that I'd taken my unborn child's chance at life away. I just couldn't. That would ruin me, the man I'd become, and everything that I morally stood for. But I can't lie and say that it wasn't considered. I was only with Dahlia for financial and family gain, and us having another baby would be an added cost that I couldn't afford. Dahlia had already made it perfectly clear that she was tired of being the breadwinner. Her refusal to help lift me up while I was down was another turn-off. Loving someone and being in love with them are two different things. I hated to admit that the latter was no longer. Dahlia was my wife; of course, I loved her. But was I in love? Again, no. Well, at least, I didn't think so. The thought of living without her wasn't as bad as the thought of living without Camisha had been. I could feel my heart breaking just by thinking about it. I didn't want that to happen, but I knew that it was something that would have to happen if I really wanted to keep my marriage together. I was just caught between a rock and a hard place. Fucking Camisha was fun, but fucking Dahlia was free. Which one served my benefit was the biggest question of all. A question that only time held the answer to.

"Stop," she said through clenched teeth. Dahlia then slammed the purple paddle brush down on the vanity table and gaped at me through the mirror. "Stop with the excuses. It sounds like you're just not too interested in going."

"Honey, I'm tired. And you know that's not my type of setting." I yawned. "Jamie also has a busy day tomorrow. Leaving her to care for Ken and Jax wouldn't be fair."

Jamie Provost was Dahlia's business-partner-turned-friend, a church counselor, and an occasional babysitter. We'd done many double-date nights out and bible studies with her and her used-to-be husband, Robert before they divorced a year ago. They still co-parented for the kids, Julia and Robert Jr., but it wasn't the same. Dahlia and I always said that we didn't want that to be us, but as of now, their situation was sort of starting to look like a reflection. Like me, Robert didn't wear the pants in his relationship. Happy wife, happy life, right? Isn't that the bullshit they've been selling us since the beginning of time? Dahlia and Jamie were so much alike that it annoyed me to be around them at the same time. They were both bossy and flossy. So high-class that you'd need a degree to hang around their grade of people. That, I didn't have, but Dahlia definitely couldn't let her scholars and scammers know that. I call them scammers because they were all living above their means.

Thankfully, I'd only have to put up with one of them tonight. Dahlia was getting honored by the City of Anniston for her hard work throughout the community, and to her, it was a must that I was in attendance. She was so great at what she did that the city often hired her to decorate a number of events that Anniston was putting together. I've always been proud of her, but it would've felt good for her to be proud of me for once. She was only proud of me when I had a penny.

Dahlia spun around and sized me up, her T-Zone covered in chalky dust. I took it that she was putting on her makeup.

"Tired? At six o'clock in the evening, you're tired? From what?" she asked, the sound of her makeup brush hitting against the plastic jar of powder making me cringe.

"Look, let's not upset the baby." I fixed my tie,

bringing it up to my neck. "I-I-I was just saying, Dah."

Dahlia's iPhone X started to ring off of the hook for the fifth or sixth time. It'd been going crazy for the last ten or fifteen minutes, but knowing her, it was probably a client vying for time that should've been set out for her family. Each time it'd ring, she'd send it to voicemail and turn it over.

"You're upsetting the baby! Not me!" she stated, opening up her jewelry box and untangling her necklaces. "We've been talking about this all month! You don't do anything else around here, so there isn't any excuse why you can't go."

"Who keeps calling your phone?" I asked, avoiding her rude comment. "Sounds like you have quite a few customers bugging you this evening."

"If you know who it is, then why ask?" Dahlia spritzed more TRESemmé.

"Because I have that right."

"Who was calling your phone?" she catechized me, deflecting it off of her. "Tell me that, Cameron."

"When?"

"Just a minute ago. Why did you have to go way out to the garage to take it?"

"Oh, that was Al."

"Al? Al who?" She slid a bulky, pearl choker around

her neck.

"The guy who had the lead on the construction job for me," I fibbed, smoothing the wrinkles out of the off-white blazer I was sporting.

"What did he say?" she perked up, placing the pearl earrings in her earlobes. "Any good news?"

"Not my cup of tea," I flatly stated, carrying the lie. Al hadn't told me anything about the job since I first inquired, so I took it that they'd found someone else who was more suitable for the position. I'd written that off a week ago. "The pay doesn't match the labor."

"Are you serious?"

"Yes, I am. It just wasn't the one for me. Better will come along, I'm sure."

She paused, looking baffled.

"So, you pass up on an opportunity that's right in front of your face because you think the pay isn't good enough for you?!" Dahlia yelled. "Judging by your current funds, any pay is good enough! How could you be so stupid?"

"I have to do what's best, Dahlia, and that just wasn't it."

The cushion in the stool, covered in gray suede, went back to its normal form as she got up and waltzed over to me.

SIDE CHICKS CATCH FEELINGS TOO

Now, nearly forehead-to-forehead, she stared me in the eyes for what felt like an eternity. Then... she smacked me. Right on the left side of my fucking face. In my damn jaw.

"The hell?!" I caught her wrist with my hand and squeezed it so tight that her circulation was probably close to being cut. "Who the hell do you think you are? Putting your hands on me? Really, Dahlia? Is that what we've come to?"

"You're a disgusting piece of shit. You deserved that," she spitefully said. "Screw you, Cameron! Stay your ass here, and sleep on the couch. I'll be damned if I let you sleep next to me tonight!"

"Dahlia!" I tried stopping her from walking out of the room, but she just kept pushing me away.

"Once you've thought about what you've done, then I may consider you coming back to the bed. Until then, suffer, you moron!" She bum-rushed her way through the bedroom entrance, slamming the door behind her. She shut that door so hard that the paintings on our wall damn near fell to the floor.

I went outside, smoked a cigarette, then watched as she and the kids retreated from the house, down the driveaway, and into Dahlia's 2019 Mercedes-Benz G-Class. That was her prized possession; it was black, with a pinked-out interior. Her favorite color. A Barbie-style car for a real-life Barbie. I ripped that tight ass tie off of my neck and sat on the bank in front of our two-story home. Legs to my chest and a blazing Newport relaxing between the tips of my index finger and thumb. I then unbuttoned my shirt, slouching my elbows on the crown of my knees. I looked at the time on my silver-plated Walmart watch; it was now 6:30 p.m. My phone had so many missed calls and unread text messages from Camisha on it that I was almost scared to open them. Thank God I'd had it on silent in front of Dahlia. I couldn't figure out why she was blowing me up when I never told her I was coming to begin with. After the shit that Dahlia had just pulled, though, it was making me rethink my first response. I buttoned my shirt back up, removed myself from the ground, and dusted my black pants off. I then walked to my 2017 Nissan Altima and fell inside. I started the engine and put my seatbelt on. The radio was still on 98.7 Kiss FM. I listened to *The Tom Joyner Morning Show* every morning like Saturday-night football, which is why it always stayed on that station. I turned the volume of it down and adjusted my rearview mirror. I grabbed my Versace glasses from the dashboard and glided them over my eyes. I then decided to call Camisha back, but she didn't answer. So, I called again. It rung three times, then she answered. She was furious that I'd kept her waiting.

 She wouldn't be waiting any longer, though. Maybe

seeing what Camisha had to say wouldn't be that bad after all.

***

By the time I'd gotten to Camisha, it was a little after seven o'clock. Summertime was here, so the light of day was still upon us. I drove along McClellan Boulevard, then turned onto 47th street, which ran between the middle school and an AutoZone. I parked in an alley at the back of the automotive parts store and walked across the way to an open space, surrounded by trees and a green electricity box that was guarded by a fence. Ahead lied a bridge. An old, corroded one that looked as if it'd been around since the Jim Crow era. I was surprised to see that it was still standing; I hadn't taken this route in so long. I was almost positive that if a branch felt on that shit, it'd crumble like wind being blown in a tent. I exited my vehicle and studied the somewhat secluded area. If I hadn't known any better, I would've thought that I was about to get my head chopped off and buried six feet under. It was spookily deserted. I didn't even know people still traveled this road until I saw a navy-blue Toyota Corolla making its way past me.

"So, we're ignoring each other now?" Camisha bustled over to me, her sneakers annoyingly crunching against the gravel. "Is that what we're doing?"

I figured she parked her Malibu in AutoZone's parking lot since that's the direction she was coming from.

"No, Misha," I said, clicking the lock button on the remote to my Altima. "I was with Dahlia and the kids. You knew that."

She glanced back at the busy highway behind us. "How was I supposed to know that?"

"Where am I when we aren't fucking, Misha?" I asked, stuffing my business phone into my back pocket. "With my family! I can't pick up when I'm around them."

"But, usually, you still answer me! You never let my calls go to voicemail without sending me a text right after," she argued. "What's up with you? If anything, I'm the one who should be acting funny with your lying ass! But I'm trying to make this work because I love you, Cameron!"

"I'm trying to make this work, too," I convinced, folding my lips into my mouth and slithering my tongue across them. "But I can't do that if you're in one ear and Dahlia's in the other! Just chill out for once!"

"How are you trying to make this work? Hmph?" She talked to me with her right finger pointed in my face as she scowled up at me. "Have you even thought about what I said? I shouldn't be the only one trying to repair what you've already broken!"

"And you're not." I rested my forehead in the palm of my left hand, the other one stationed on my waist. I just wished she'd calm down and let me say what I'd come here to say.

"You know what? I don't even know why I'm still trying! I should just give up. You shouldn't have gotten the bitch pregnant, period. This is all your fault!" she blamed, laughing as the tears crawled down her full cheeks. "You knew this would hurt me, but you're standing there like you don't care! I'm tired of getting hurt!"

"I never meant to hurt you!" The sound of the steady traffic began to override my voice, prompting me to talk louder. "I love you, Camisha! I love you so fucking much, which makes this even harder!"

"If you loved me, then you wouldn't mind getting Dahlia out of the damn picture! She serves you no good, so why does it matter?"

"It matters to my kids, Misha. Don't you understand that? Do you even have a heart anymore?" I lowered my tone, now able to hear her clearly.

She didn't say anything. She twisted her bottom lip upward and to the side, rolling her eyes.

"Look..." I added. "I don't want to lose you, Misha."

"Then start acting like it," she said, searching my

eyes with hers. "Do what's needed for us to stay together."

I removed the sunglasses from my face and relaxed my broad shoulders. "It's not that simple."

"You keep saying that!" She stumbled back, dropping her hands to her waist. "Why isn't it 'that simple?'"

Dahlia was the source for everything. Lights in our home, food on our table, clothes on our backs, and gas in our cars. Without Dahlia, neither of us, Camisha nor myself, would be able to live comfortably. Hell, maybe not even live at all. I should've just been honest from the jump and told Camisha about the drop in my income, but I was afraid that if I did, she'd look at me differently and walk away. Like Dahlia had been doing. Things changed when I lost my job. I had the chance to see a side of Dahlia that I'd never seen before; she was greedy and selfish. Dahlia was only okay with pulling her weight as long as I was pulling mine. She helped me get on my feet, but once she did, she expected me to stand on my own and never have to fall back on her again. It's kind of idiotic, especially since we're in a marriage, and that's what marriage is about. Having a person to rely on—a partner. She wasn't that great of a team player, and lately, I've been learning that. Wealth won her over, and I lost the woman I'd once known and loved. In her book, everything needed to be equal. She was an Alpha female who'd been raised to sit pretty on her throne while the king fends for himself. Nothing's wrong with that, but what about when the king's crown starts to fall? Isn't that what his queen is for? To help him readjust it? And vice versa? Before we got married, I mentioned the idea of a prenup, but she was against it. Now that we're a decade in and circumstances are different, a postnup wouldn't be so bad. But I knew she wouldn't agree to that either, so I didn't bother to bring it up. It wouldn't be fair for either of us to walk away with nothing. Don't get me wrong; I still believe in being the man of the house, taking care of my woman and my family, but life just hadn't been fair to me over these past few months. Shit has gotten tough, and it made me feel less than a man to not be able to get through it as fast as I would've liked to. Where I used to be and where I am now is fucked up. I couldn't even take care of myself, so how was I going to take care of Camisha? I couldn't keep this secret from her any longer, though. The quicker I got it off my chest, the better I'd feel.

"I'm broke, Misha. Broke! Okay?!" I blurted out. "So broke that I'm stuck in a marriage that I really don't want to be in."

"Broke?" She laughed, not believing a word that'd just flown from my mouth. "If you want to cut me off, just say that. Be a man about it instead of trying to lie! That has nothing to do with this! You know it's never been about the money with me."

"I'm not lying," I told her. "Dahlia is my income. I lost my job months ago!"

"Months ago?" she pressed, watching my lips as they moved. "Cameron, really? Where are you going with this?"

"I wanted to tell you, but I could never find the right time to do it or the right way to say it." I choked up, clearing my throat. "Dahlia's been paying for everything."

"Everything like what?"

"Your bills and ours."

"I knew it! I knew she knew about us." Camisha stood in astonishment. "She's content with sharing you, but she's trying to do everything she can to keep you there! Like having that damn baby! And paying your mistress off!"

"No, no, no," I replied. "She thinks I'm spending the money on gambling. She doesn't know anything about you. How many times do I have to say that?"

"Gambling?" The laugh came again. This time harder than the first one. "Wow, so naïve."

"I'm sorry, Camisha. I should've told you, but—"

She interrupted me with a tongue-pulling, lip-biting kiss then excitedly said, "So, this is what you've been depressed about?"

"Pretty much, yes." I side-eyed her, suspiciously

watching her. Surprisingly, she was warm and sweet, as if she hadn't just found out that I'd gotten my supposedly 'estranged' wife pregnant and been using Dahlia's money to take care of her expenses.

"And this is why you haven't gotten divorced?"

"Part of the reason. Not all of it," I fessed up.

"I wasn't with you for your money, Cameron. I was with you because I loved you and still do." She kissed me again, whispering against my lips. "This is perfect."

"How? Hmph? Tell me how the fuck this could be any ounce of perfect, Misha," I grilled. "I've gotten myself in a hole that I can't get out of."

"Remember that big-ass insurance policy you once told me about," Camisha brought up, chewing on some Twizzlers that she pulled from her pocket. "Handle her, then you'll be set, babe. We'll be set, without her. See, problem solved!"

"She's carrying my child."

"It's barely even a damn seed," she cold-heartedly said. "Think about yourself for once, Cameron. Dahlia doesn't give two damns about you. She'd do it to you in a heartbeat. Look at it that way."

"I don't think she would," I defended. "I'm the father of her children."

"After how you told me she talks to you?" Camisha

giggled. "You really think she wouldn't jump on the first opportunity to take you the fuck out? Aren't you tired of that? This is your chance! This is your way out, babe."

"Maybe you're right," I scaled back.

"I know I am," she confidently responded. "So, are you in or out?"

She got me. I shifted my eyes to the sky, amazed by the brilliance of this woman. *Jack-motherfucking-pot.* Through all of this, I hadn't even thought about the life insurance policies that Dahlia and I had taken out a few months ago. We were the beneficiary of each other's. $100,000. It amused me how Dahlia agreed to that but couldn't agree to a prenup. I guess the money wouldn't matter when she was dead.

I looked across the street then back to Camisha. "Alright. Okay, I'm in, but under one condition."

Your kids, Cameron. Think about your kids, I kept trying to tell myself. But I couldn't bring myself to listen to that. Who was I turning into?

"What is that?" she asked eagerly.

"I don't want any parts in the actual crime. I want my hands clean."

"And they will be. Just trust me," Camisha assured me. "I have a guy who can get the job done for twenty thousand."

"Twenty? Nah, see if he can take ten or fifteen," I negotiated. "That's feasible."

"Ten or fifteen? Ehhh, I don't know about that," she sighed, squinting her eyes from the beaming sunset. "I'll see what I can do."

"Let's meet here tomorrow. Same time?" I recommended. "We have some things to map out."

"That'll work." She began to tread to her car, but I stopped her.

"And, hey..." I pinched her juicy-ass forearm.

"Yes?" A puzzled expression washed across her face.

"Just keep my children safe and out of this, please."

"You don't have to worry about that." She winked, tapping the bottom of my chin with her finger before parting ways.

CHAPTER SIX

CAMISHA "MISHA" ATKINS

"Misha-Mish!" My loud-mouth, Spades-playing, Henny-drinking brother, Dominic, yelled, walking out of the house as soon as I pulled into the yard. He held his tatted arms up in the air, waving his hands from side to side. "What's good, sis?"

The crowd of fellas stared at me, faint mumblings leaving their breaths. There were five-to-six dudes on Dominic's porch, standing in a circle—drinking, smoking and shooting dice. I killed the music I was playing. Mary J. Blige's *Strength of a Woman* album was the bomb. She never seemed to let me down. Dominic stood under the gray-and-black awning for a second as if he was awaiting me to join them. He knew not to ask me to get out because that wasn't happening. Especially not with his homeboy, Reggie, up there. The fool still owed me twenty dollars from three weeks ago. And he'd been trying to fuck me for as long as I could remember. He was one of those who didn't take rejection well. I was the plus-sized sister all of my brothers' friends secretly dreamed about but were too afraid of what their niggas would think to showcase it. It didn't make me any never mind. It wasn't like I wanted them. They were all broke, ugly, and only changed clothes every two days. But screenshots never lie. At least, not mine.

"Nothing too much, Dom," I hollered out of the window. "Come here for a minute."

"You ain't getting out?" he asked disappointingly. I don't know why; he knew this wasn't my type of scene. "Tiffany's in the house."

Tiffany was my brother's girlfriend of three years. She was a slim, young thing. Dark-skinned like Dominic. Just turned twenty-two, with the whole world at her fingertips. Boy, don't I wish I could go back to those days. Had I known what I know now, I probably would've been dumped Cameron's ass a long time ago, then I wouldn't be in this shit I'm in now. In love and willing to do anything to stay in it.

I gave him 'the look.' He knew what that meant. *Hell no.*

"No, I can't right now."

Dominic's red-and-white Alabama hat was turned to the back, with the tag still attached to it. His Sean John Flight Cargo shorts were damn near mowing the lawn and sweeping the sidewalk. They were tan-colored and sagging. His blue Polo Ralph Lauren boxers made a special appearance. If it hadn't been for the belt, of the same brand, saving his bottoms from falling, all of his business would've been fully exposed. He wore a gold chain around his neck and a big silver watch on his wrist. He was serious about his swagger, thinking he was doing something every time he stepped out of the house and into the hood. Unlike his friends, my brother stayed fresh. Though his style was stuck in 2006, he still looked nice and smelled good. Not a wrinkle in his white T-shirt or a mud streak on his Jordan shoes to be seen. At 5'4" and a half and twenty-eight years old, my big, little brother was the life of the party and of the family. He was a Quarter boy through and through. We grew up on Cobb Avenue, better known as 'The Quarters,' and Dominic still lived over this way. As did our parents. This may have been a small community, but it was home. It was our neighborhood, our stomping grounds. Too low for the high-class but just enough for us. Daddy always made sure that there was food in the freezer, and Mama did her best to keep it on the table. Our childhood wasn't lavish, but it was loving. Despite Mama and Daddy's ruling, eighty-twenty relationship and strict household dynamics, there was no doubt in our minds that they loved us and cared for us. I'd say they raised us well. None of us had any real issues. Well, that we knew of. I don't know about Dominic, though. He stayed in and out of trouble, and his criminal record was about the same length as an encyclopedia. Gratefully, all misdemeanors or things that would eventually fall off. But I knew that if anyone could get the job done for Cameron and me, it'd be him. Dominic didn't mind doing the dirty work, especially if it was for his baby sister.

He trudged out to my car and leaned forward, bringing me in for a hug. "What's up? You good?" asked Dominic.

"Get in."

"For what?" he stalled.

"Just get in, fool," I told him, snatching my purse off of the floor to put it in the backseat. "I need to talk business."

His bow-legged ass came around the front of the vehicle and went to the passenger's side to get in.

"What you on, Misha?" he questioned. "You ain't ever just popped up at my crib unannounced."

"Is it a problem?" I posed. "Because I can leave."

"Nah, you straight. But tell me what's up. You scaring your brother, baby," he worriedly said. "Do I need to fuck somebody up? Cameron did something to you? He put his hands on you? Hmph?"

"Calm down, Dom. Damn." I laughed. He'd go to war for me. See, this would be easy. "Cameron didn't put his hands on me. That's first. Secondly, let me talk."

"Alright, go ahead. Spit it out, girl." He stuffed the strings hanging from his white durag, which was tied around his head, back underneath his hat. "I know you, and I don't need no damn surprises."

I chuckled. "I need you, Dom."

"Need me for what?" He fingered his chin hairs, sizing me up with his dark-brown pupils. His eyeballs were a lightly-tinted yellow, which turned red whenever he'd get angry. He needed to stop all that drinking and cutting up. It was declining his health.

"I have something that needs to be taken care of, and we could get paid big-time if it's done right," I began to go over the details.

"Okay, like what? How big we talking?"

"Thousands."

"Word?" His eyes bucked. "What I gotta do?"

I moved around in my seat, nervous to see what his response would be. "I need you to take someone out for me."

"The fuck?!?!" He jumped, holding on to the door handle as if he wanted to run out. "Sis, you serious? Now, wait, wait, wait a damn minute now. I know this ain't my Misha-Mish talking like this."

I hadn't asked him to harm anyone since that Brandon dude from high school. The one who I gave my virginity to. I was so infuriated after the shit that he pulled, so I got Dominic to beat his ass. He'd done so much damage to that boy that it was a wonder he didn't catch his first murder charge then.

"Just hear me out, Dom," I tried to explain. "There's a reason behind this."

"What good reason could you possibly have for wanting to kill somebody?" he asked discreetly. "I've done a lot of shit in my lifetime, but this? Oh, hell nah."

"Cameron got his wife pregnant."

"And? Don't they already have kids together? And aren't they *still* married?" he nonchalantly threw it up in my face. "I told you before all of this shit got too deep to let that nigga go. But you didn't listen. What does this have to do with what you're asking me to do anyway?"

"I want you to get Dahlia out of the way for me."

"What?!"

"You don't understand, Dom," I refuted. "Just try to see things from my point of view. I didn't even know they were still sleeping together... as husband and wife. I thought their relationship was just a roommate type of set up. I'm the one who's feeling fucking played."

"*I* don't understand? No, *you* don't understand. That roommate shit is always a lie. I know because I'm a man myself, and I've said that same shit but still be fucking the bitch I claim I can't stand," Dominic expressed. "I'm not about to get caught up in some shit like this with you. You on your own with this, sis. If you mad at anybody, it should be him."

Out of all of my brothers, Derrick, Barry, J.R., and Dominic, I couldn't trust any of the others like I trusted Dominic. We were closer in age, and we related in ways that I couldn't relate to the older ones. They had no clue that I had been Cameron's side chick for all these years, and I had no intention of them finding out. Mama and Daddy didn't know either. They just knew that Cameron was older, which was where their issue came in. 'He's too old for you, Cammy,' Mama would advise. 'He's mature; he's experienced some things you haven't experienced. You're not ready for that.' That'd only go in one ear and out of the other. Dominic knew because I knew he wouldn't judge me as much, and he was too busy fucking his own life up to try to fuck mine up. He couldn't care less about what I was doing, as long as I was happy. I used to be. Now, I was too hurt to be happy. But getting Dahlia's ass out of the way would make me happy again. I'd have Cameron, and we'd have her money. Again, it's never been solely about the money for me, but I can't say that I wouldn't enjoy going to the bank and cashing those coins.

"What if I could get you twenty thousand?" I offered, hoping that'd butter Dominic up. "Twenty thousand dollars! You'd be a fool to pass that up."

"That's sick, Camisha. Do you realize how you sound right now?"

"Keep it down. Your friends are out there," I said through clenched teeth. "It's not sick. It's payback. I don't care what Cameron says; that bitch knows about me, and she's trying to keep him from me, completely. That's why she got pregnant. She knows how soft he is when it comes to his kids."

"So, you're willing to risk your freedom for that bullshit? You sound dumb."

"Do you know what you could do with twenty thousand dollars? You could get a new car, instead of riding around in that old-ass Cutlass that Daddy gave you when you were seventeen!" I laid it on thick. "You could spoil Tiffany, take her on a shopping spree. Stash some money away for little Dominique. Finally get out of the hood. You could do a lot with that, Dom."

"Little Dominique?"

"I know you and Tiffany have been talking about popping out a baby for the longest," I mentioned. "But you've never had the right finances to do so. Now is your chance."

"Twenty thousand would only go so far," Dominic commented, looking straight ahead. He couldn't bring himself to look at me. "It's not worth it, Misha. I'm good with my job at the foundry."

"It is worth it! You won't be able to work at Honda forever! And you've told me how damaging it is to your back!"

"It's not worth my freedom! Besides, where is this money coming from?" He took a sip from his stacked Styrofoam cups. "I'm trying to walk a straight line, Misha. Stop trying to fuck that up for me!"

"I know, Dom. I know, but you can't do this one favor for me? No one's going to get caught if it's gone about the proper way. His wife has a hundred-thousand-dollar life insurance policy. If she dies, it immediately goes to Cameron."

"What does that have to do with you?" he continued on with his twenty-one questions. "He's in on this?"

"Yep. Of course, he'd share the money with me, and I'd pay the hitman," I said.

"I don't know about this, Misha. It just doesn't feel right."

"What doesn't feel right?"

"You going to these lengths to keep a man who

doesn't want to be kept."

"He doesn't want to be kept by Dahlia. That's the problem," I clarified. "He loves me."

"How do you know that?"

"Dahlia has been making his life a living hell since he lost his job a few months ago."

It brought joy to me to know that I'd gotten Cameron on my side, where he should've been all along. And it didn't take nearly as long as I thought it would. I'd gotten him to meet with me after I left lunch with Mimi yesterday. I was so convinced that he wasn't going to show up, but after playing house and hubby with Dahlia for the day, he finally showed. All it took was for him to marinate on that head I'd given him a few days ago. He was also probably thinking about the quick cash he'd get from Dahlia's policy, too. I remembered him telling me that Dahlia had taken out an insurance policy during another one of his venting sessions about her, and that was a vital piece of information that I said I would never let go of. He's told me so much about Dahlia that it was like I knew her personally, but that's neither here nor there.

To be frank, I'd been thinking about offing Dahlia for quite a while, but I never really had a valid reason to because I was trying to be content with the way that things were going between Cameron and I. The pregnancy blew the top off the lid for me, though. That was it. Because I knew that this was done out of spite. Something in my gut was telling me that what Cameron and I had was no longer a secret to her, and she was trying her best to win the competition. But I had news for that bitch. Cameron wasn't no saint, though. I couldn't believe he'd lied to me about not having a job, but it made a bitch feel like she meant something to know that he was lying to Dahlia's ass about where her money was going to keep my bills paid.

"So, that's what this is about? It's about the money?" Dominic huffed, his chest sinking inward. "If he doesn't have a job, how has he been keeping up your apartment?"

"No, no, no. Not just that," I stopped him. "And he's been getting money from her to help me. I don't want him to have to do that anymore."

"Look, I don't know what kind of sick-ass shit y'all got going on, but it needs to stop. Does she know that's where her money has been going?"

"I'm not so sure. Cameron says she doesn't."

"So, if it's not about the money for y'all, what is it about?" My brother proceeded to question me.

"He's tired of her. He wants out, and I'm trying to save him... save us. I'm not ready to let him go. I love him, and I'm tired of sharing."

"Well, he should've gotten the divorce that he's seven years late for!"

"Enough, Dom. Cut him some slack," I encouraged. "This hurt me, and I was upset. But everybody makes mistakes."

"Yeah, but once muthafuckas start making that same mistake over and over again, they eventually learn some shit. How you gon' forgive a nigga overnight for some shit like this?"

"Did you learn when you kept cheating on Tiffany last year? And didn't she forgive you?"

"This ain't about me, Misha," he deflected. "This is about you and this crazy-ass shit you trying to get me involved in."

As much as I hated to admit it, my brother was telling the truth. What Cameron did was wrong, but we had a chance to make this right. I'd been had it out for this Dahlia bitch for a long time, and I was tired of living my life with Cameron in secret. If she's gone, we won't have to hide this shit. If it was left up to me, I would've been outed us, but I always thought of Cameron. He was so afraid of Dahlia finding out about us that he'd done everything in his power to keep us away from each other. He'd almost gotten caught up a couple of times, but not for long. He was an expert at wiggling himself out of sticky situations. Cameron was smooth, sneaky. He knew just the words to say and how to play them. Gosh, I hated how hard I'd fallen for that two-timing, conniving muthafucka. He could've been grown the balls to toss Dahlia in the trash like the used goods she was. But, instead, this was something that I had to do... for both of us. Maybe then, I'd get a ring and a baby.

I snapped from my thoughts and back into reality, clamping my hands around the hot steering wheel. My fingers kept opening and closing.

"You're right. I shouldn't have brought that up, but still." I looked through the rearview mirror to see a group of children riding their bicycles down the street. "No one could ever understand what Cameron and I have. It's real, and I've invested too much into thi—"

"I'm gucci. Find someone else for the job. Matter of that, don't even do it," Dominic said. "This shit is beyond me, man. I can't believe you."

"You can't tell me what to do. No one would get caught. Dahlia's going to disappear, and we'd be rich! Do you hear me? Rich!" I hugged him.

He gently pushed me off of him. "This shit just doesn't sit well with me. Killing a pregnant bitch? Really?"

"We're meeting with Cameron this evening to talk more about it."

"We? Ain't no fucking 'we.' I haven't agreed to shit. I know you ain't going to his house?"

"No, a discreet location."

"What time?" he asked, peering down at his timepiece.

"Around eight. Your raggedy friends should be gone by then," I joked. "And I'm sure you don't have anything else to do."

"Why you getting on my boys like that?" Dominic laughed. "And you don't know what my schedule looks like. Either way, it doesn't include this shit."

"Yeah, yeah, yeah. Because I can," I comically said, shooing him away. "So, are you in or what?"

He took a few seconds to respond as if he was doing some serious thinking.

"I just told you I'm gucci." I thought that he, of all people, would actually do it, but I was wrong.

"Get the fuck out of my car," I shouted. "Since it's obvious that you're not on my side."

"Man, whatever. You know I'm here for you, Mish. But this? Nah. Don't do no crazy shit. Leave that muthafucka and his wife alone."

Alone?

"Bye, Dom. You can go now."

"Bye," he replied. "Don't get yourself in nothing you

can't get yourself out of."

Yeah, sure. Like I'm going to listen to you?

Dominic scratched the dry skin around the patches of eczema that covered each of his cheeks, grabbed his cup of Lean, and shot out of the Malibu and back up on his porch. With a head nod and a peace sign, he fell back into one of the brown folding chairs that sat on the stoop and watched his friends bicker and banter over who won the last round of dice. "Man, nawl! You know that ain't right!" I heard in passing. "On my mama, I got that one! Give me my props!" Reggie's big-mouth behind antagonized. He was 5'5" with the confidence of a man who was 6'5". Slender-built with loose man titties that looked like pig noses, medium-brown, and black-gummed. Yet, he still had three baby mamas and one in questioning. Oddly, it's usually the dustiest ones with the most to show for themselves. *I'll never understand.*

I was mad and disappointed at Dominic's reluctance. I didn't bother tooting the horn as I rode past his one-bedroom shack that, on a daily, everybody in the neighborhood treated as a five-bedroom palace. My brother lived in a dead-end, near a church, and only a few doors down from Mama and Daddy. Something told me to stop, but this wouldn't be the first time I didn't... if I hadn't. I'd be lying if I said I didn't miss my mother's touch or my father's protection, but that was a chapter of my life that had closed, and my story was still being written. With or without them.

    I looked out of the window, noticing that the flowers in front of my parents' home still bloomed as beautifully as they did the last time that I'd taken a moment to smell them. Which was two years ago, on Christmas Day, right before Daddy told me to 'take my stupid ass back over there with that negro and don't come back, ever again.' Dominic had begged me to come over, and I did, but just as I thought, it turned into an episode of *Oprah's Lifeclass*. I was tired of battling with them. Even though I wasn't living under their roof anymore, they felt compelled to dictate the dick that I was getting. That's when I officially cut them off, and unlike any other time, I told myself that I was done. Some things just aren't meant to be fixed, and they're better off broken. But, like today, there were many days where I longed for a good cry in Jeanie Atkins' arms. You know, those cries that scream help and can only be rescued by a woman who's cried them before and knows just what to do or say to dry them: Mama. But life goes on, and everybody just can't go with you. Family members can be just as toxic as a bitch on the street.

    The windows were cracked and the wind was coming in heavy. My hair soared backward, rays stinging the center of my face as I drove head-on with the sun. I should've borrowed my brother's sunshade to put in my windshield, but oh, well. I quickly put the thoughts of my parents behind me and cruised away. Those thoughts were replaced with newer ones, scarier ones. Even through all of the pain, I was still human, and I still felt. Something I hadn't been able to do since I'd found out about Dahlia's pregnancy. I began second-guessing, wondering if what I was about to do was right or wrong. To me, it was right because Cameron had done me wrong too many times on the account of Dahlia. And it was wrong because two wrongs simply don't make a right. But, again, I was hurting. Dahlia wasn't going to walk away at her own free will. Like me, she'd given so much of herself to this man. Even if it was only two-going-on-three kids and a lifestyle created on lies. She wasn't going to give him up so easily. But, after today, she would have no choice.

I was now driving into Mata's Greek Pizza's parking lot on Quintard Avenue. It was hard to believe that this building used to be a Hardees and that their old building was across the street, next to a used-to-be Chinese restaurant. My, how times have changed... and even the city. I was happy that they'd moved, though. The parking was better and the dining area was larger. I'd been craving a pan of their spaghetti with extra cheese, add peppers, onions, and mushrooms. I couldn't forget the meat sauce. Just the way I like it. I went inside to order, told them what I wanted, and I waited as the guys behind the counter prepared my food. I said "what's up" to Rock; I knew him from The Quarters. He always kept a job and had been working here for a while. He was a cool guy and, at one point, he and Dominic were the best of friends.

"Camisha, is that you?" he yelled from the kitchen, pulling the pizzas from the oven. His dreads seemed to get longer and longer every time I'd see him. "How you living?"

"Hey, Rock! I'm good. How's everything with you?" I inquired, standing off to the side and crossing my hands over my tummy. "How are the kids?"

"Everything's straight! They good. I been asking your brother, Dominic, about you."

"Oh, yeah? Dominic hadn't said a thing about that," I chatted. "That damn boy..."

"His old ass probably suffering from memory loss," Rock talked shit and tee-heed. "Yeah, I was wondering where you been at. Ain't seen you in a minute."

"I still be in The Quarters… very seldom, but I come through. What about you?"

"Oh, for real? Same." He whisked closer to the side that I was standing on, untying the messy work apron from around his neck. "Where you staying now?"

"Fox Valley."

"Oh, yeah, yeah. I remember you telling me that the last time I bumped into you at the Chevron on fifteenth," Rock said, dusting flour from his black tee. "How you like it over there?"

"Actually, it's cool. I stay to myself, so I'm good anywhere."

"I feel you on that," he agreed. "Got to nowadays. Shit crazy out here in these streets."

"Yeah, people getting shot at and places getting shot up."

"Damn right. That's exactly why I go to work and come home," he stated. "I don't be out here like I used to be. A lot has changed, Mish."

"I see!" I fixed the strap to the crossbody bag that was choking my neck.

"Let me stop running my mouth. I think your spaghetti is ready." Rock smacked the countertop before walking away from it and back into the kitchen.

The restaurant was occupied to capacity. Some workers roamed the dining floor, cleaning tables and sweeping, while others stayed in the kitchen rolling dough, dressing pizzas, and making salads. Customers were visiting the tables and busying the registers. A lot of them had kids with them who wore the biggest smiles, strings of cheese, and marinara sauce on their faces; a few with significant others too focused on their phones to pay any ounce of attention to the person who sat before them. It's a damn shame how much technology had invaded our lives. We couldn't even enjoy a date with our partner without picking up our cell phones—and, in some cases, turning it over and putting it back down. Just the other week, I was at Olive Garden with Cameron and we were sitting next to this Caucasian couple. She was trying her hardest to keep him involved in the subject at hand: her, but his Galaxy Note must've held something of more importance. I could see how sad she was through her misty eyes. The craziest part about it was, they both had on wedding rings. I imagined that's how dinner with Dahlia looked for Cameron.

A few minutes later, Rock packaged my food and brought it to me. Before I left, I told him to keep in touch. Not on any funny business, but family business. He was one of my brother's friends who I could actually tolerate. It was good to see someone I'd practically grown up with. These days, I rarely come in contact with anyone I know from The Quarters. I'd been living in my own little bubble with Cameron for the past seven years and hadn't had time to see what was going on in everyone else's.

I opened the driver's door to my car and got in. I sat there for a moment, taking in the aroma of the freshly-cooked spaghetti that I couldn't wait to have a forkful of. I declined Mimi's calls; she didn't want anything. I knew she'd be cursing me out my voicemail, but I didn't give a damn. My Bridgestone tires began beating Mata's parking lot as I was in transit to the main road.

What the fuck? I said aloud when I saw Dahlia marching across the street, arm-in-arm, with a guy who certainly wasn't Cameron. They looked as if they'd just come out of the Hotel Finial. She was showing more teeth than she'd shown in her and Cameron's wedding photos, and the unknown man was licking his lips as if he was the Hispanic version of LL Cool J. Dahlia was dressed down, with that just-got-the-dick hair. You know, frizzy and not exactly in place. She was wearing a blue jean boyfriend shirt with high-waisted shorts. It looked as if she'd borrowed ole dude's shirt and thrown on a pair of her own shorts with it. They were comfortable, and I was almost positive that this was the we-just-stayed-the-night-with-each-other type of comfortable.

I flipped the sun visor down, hoping they wouldn't see me. Well, hoping she wouldn't. I circled the parking lot, trying to see where they were headed. I initially assumed that they were going in Matas, but they walked across the way to a nearby Pic 'n Sav grocery store. Ironically, the same one I'd met Cameron in, but back then, it was a Piggly Wiggly. I

SIDE CHICKS CATCH FEELINGS TOO

opened my lock screen, pulled up the phone's camera, and took a shot of Dahlia and her new lover.

Cameron needed to see this.

CHAPTER SEVEN

CAMERON "CAM" DARGAN

Dahlia hadn't been home since yesterday, and up until I'd gotten this text message from Camisha, I was actually sort of worried about her cheating ass. Considering Jamie had a long day ahead, she brought Kennedy and Jaxon back around ten last night. She said that Dahlia was going to be a little late coming back from the honorary banquet and had told her to go ahead and bring them so I could get them in bed. Dahlia never returned. I put Ken and Jax to sleep and tried calling and texting their mother but got nothing. I took it as she'd probably stayed over at her other girlfriend, Victoria's, house because she was still upset that I hadn't gone with her to the dinner. Or, I thought maybe she'd slept in her car—like she'd done on quite a few occasions after a disagreement. But, now, it was all starting to make sense as to why she'd suddenly up and leave whenever we'd get into an argument. She'd use them as excuses to go be a whore. She was dropping us like fish in a hot fryer and cozying up with somebody else who meant more to her than her fucking family. It made me wonder if those weekends she'd run off to her parents' in Atlanta was just a lie to cover the truth. The truth that she'd been going and laying up with that sad-ass simp. It also made me question if that baby was mine. I would've never imagined that I'd have to do that with the woman I was married to. It was even more disgusting to think about her continuing to do this shit while carrying. I couldn't believe that my wife was stepping out on me, and who would've thought that my side chick would be the one to tell me about it? I was just finishing up a pot of Ramen noodles for the kids when my phone lit up with a notification from Camisha. There were three attachments, and they were all photos of Dahlia and Jamie's ex-husband, Robert, who I mentioned earlier. They were locking hands and seemingly dancing through the streets like they were on an episode of *Dancing with the Stars*.

"Daddy, you're burning our food!" yelled Kennedy. It was hard to keep my composure and focus on the task at hand. I turned the stovetop off. Just about all of the water had drained out of the noodles. Smoke flailed from the boiler of crispy Ramen, and I coughed and fanned in reaction.

"Fuck!!!!" I screamed, squirming profusely and dropping the large serving spoon I had in my hand. My fingertips were on fire from touching the hot rim of the pot. I ran them under cold water, hoping that'd give me some relief.

"Are you okay, Daddy?" Jaxon fluttered.

No, I'm not okay. Your tramp of a mother is cheating on me and out here making me look weaker than I already feel, I wanted to say, but instead, I said, "Yeah, yeah. I'm okay. Looks like we'll be having cereal for lunch, since your mother isn't here, and I don't know what the heck I'm doing."

"Aw, man! We ate that for breakfast! I don't want that; I want noodles, Daddy!" Kennedy was moody and petulant. Her attitude was just like Dahlia's, even though she was the spitting image of me, with a big-ass forehead, chinky eyes, and a mouth full of teeth. She was my pretty brown girl with the pretty puffy hair.

"Unless you want to wait until your mommy gets here, you won't have a choice," I sternly told my baby girl, supporting my lower back against the oven door. The heat from the stove began to burn my skin a little, so I inched away from it. "And get down off of that table and sit on the stool. I don't want you to hurt yourself!"

Kennedy and Jaxon both trembled at the amount of bass in my voice. I rarely ever yelled at my children, but I was pissed the fuck off at Dahlia. So, she was to blame.

It pissed me off, even more, to see her staggering through the door as if she hadn't been taking a piece of

SIDE CHICKS CATCH FEELINGS TOO

Spanish dick down her throat and in her guts all night. *The betrayal.* At least I'd tried to keep my affair hidden. She was prancing around parts of town where she knows she could easily be seen and didn't seem to give one fuck about it. How could she do this? Our marriage was already broken up enough. Might as well end this shit, since neither of us seemed to be honoring our vows. I might have been doing my own thing too, but she didn't know that. What if I wasn't cheating? She would still be doing this shit. This is probably why she had been dogging me out for a while now. Robert was getting her at her best, and me? I got nothing. She was doing the bare minimum to hold us together, again not giving a fuck if I'd gotten the worst. Even if I didn't necessarily vibe with Dahlia romantically anymore, as contradictory as it may sound, I still thought that we were better than that. We were friends before anything else. She could've had the common decency to tell me she didn't want this anymore. Her telling me would've made this shit with Camisha a lot easier, and I wouldn't have felt as guilty about falling for her. But, clearly, Dahlia didn't know anything about friendship. She'd been screwing the father of her close friend's children and, from the looks of it, didn't feel bad at all. This was a man who was supposedly like a brother to both of us, at one point, and this is what she goes out and does? This hurt my ego, but it would hurt more than that for Jamie.

"Mommy!!!!" The children jumped down from the bar stools and bombarded Dahlia with hugs as soon as she appeared in the doorway. She still had on the same dress she'd left in yesterday.

"Hey, my babies!" said Dahlia, kissing them on the cheek. "Did y'all miss me?"

"Yes!!!!"

"I missed y'all, too," she untruthfully replied. She couldn't have missed them. She hadn't even called to check on them. Well, other than her calling Jamie and telling her to drop them back off to me last night. "Hey, who wants to play hide-and-seek?"

"Me!" Jaxon bounced his feet from the floor in excitement. "Me! Me! Me!"

"No, me!" Kennedy got in front of her brother. "I want to play first!"

"We can play together, baby," Dahlia reasoned, kneeling to their level.

"Jaxon always gets to play with us, Mommy. Can't he play with Daddy?" Kennedy asked innocently. "He's such a pest!"

"Be nice, Ken-Ken. Your brother can play, too," I spoke from the kitchen as I emptied the remainder of the inedible noodles in the trash. Noticing that the last bit of them was stuck to the cookware, I grabbed a butter knife from the dish rack and scraped the bottom of it. "It's more fun that way."

Kennedy poked her lip out and folded her arms.

"Yes, your dad's right," Dahlia said, dramatically fainting on the couch. "Go hide! I'm coming to get you!"

The kids both smiled and happily stormed up the stairs to go do as their mother told them.

"Go! Go! Go! The last one up is a rotten egg!" Dahlia cheered, kicking her heels off her feet and lying in a fetal position.

After the babies were gone, I went to join her on the sofa. Her makeup had worn off, and so had the wand curls in her hair. Her blue eyes were low, breath was smelly. Dick. That's what was on her breath. Robert's dick.

"Where were you last night?" I gave it to her. "It's going on noon, and you're just now making it in?"

"I stayed at Victoria's after the dinner. I was too tired to make it home," she lied, sitting up and clamping her stomach with her arms. "No biggie. What's it to you anyway?"

"Everything," I said. "You're a married woman, and you're pregnant! You have no business staying out all night, Dahlia."

She laughed at me. As if I was the biggest joke of the

century. Then, she fell back into the sectional's pillows... unbothered.

"I didn't know you were my father," Dahlia retorted with closed eyes, idling her face on the back of her hands, which were lapped upon one another. "Go get a job, then you can tell me what I have no business doing. Maybe then you could also be a real man and a real father around here."

Now, it was my turn to laugh. I wanted to hit this bitch with my good hand, but Kennedy and Jaxon would've heard it.

"The funny thing is, you have a job but still find time to cheat on me with your friend's ex-husband," I commented back. "The nerve of you!"

"What?" Her body shot up. Her eyes opened and a frown began to show. "See, I should've listened to my parents when they told me how dumb you are!"

"Oh, so I'm the dumb one? No, you are! For thinking you'd never get caught!" I jerked my neck with every word that I said. I was furious. "Whose baby is it, hmph?! I know you've been fucking around with Robert!"

Spit flew from my mouth. So many emotions were erupting from my soul. My cup was overflowing, and not so much in a good way either. I felt a sense of pain and peace. It was like an "aha" moment. Dahlia had been doing the same shit all along, yet I'd programmed myself to feel bad for what I was doing? Really? That was where I got peace. But the pain came from feeling like a wimp. Maybe she was right; I wasn't a real man. Hell, I couldn't even keep the ring on my wife's finger or food in the refrigerator. It was that feeling of someone getting one up on me; I couldn't stand it. But if I'd just called it quits on Dahlia years ago and married Camisha, all of this could've been avoided. Had I known that she was creeping, too, I would've. Something had to give. Right now, it wasn't even about killing her so that I could be with Misha... it was about regaining my manhood. With Dahlia's insurance money, I could open that carpeting business I'd always wanted to get off the ground. I'd be set. A part of me was hoping she'd say that it was Robert's baby. That way, I wouldn't feel so bad watching someone slit her throat or put a bullet in her head. I needed that $100,000, and I was going to get it. She didn't care about me, so why should I have cared about her? Something snapped in me, and at this very moment, I didn't give a damn if my kids had a mother or not.

"Robert? Jamie's ex-husband? Are you fucking kidding me, Cameron?!" Dahlia fixed the padding in her dress.

"Mommy, we're waiting!!!" Jaxon hollered from the upper level.

"Coming!" she responded, hoisting up off of the

candy-red leather couch. I'd bought that one the same time I bought Camisha's. "We'll talk about this later!"

Sure, we will.

***

I looked at Camisha. "So, how are we getting this done?"

She and her brother, Dominic, and I were all gathered in my vehicle, windows up and stereo off. We were in the same meeting place as the other day, behind the AutoZone. Camisha and I were in the front, and her brother was in the back. I'd never been this close up on Dominic, but I could tell, just by looking at him, that he didn't play any games and expected none to be played in return. He was a thug, like the dope boys I used to hang with when I was a young cat. There was no doubt in my mind that he could off Dahlia's ass, and, hopefully, without a trace.

I did a 360, taking in the environment around us. The ambience was even creepier back here, with it being nighttime, but I didn't sweat it. We had some business to discuss and moves to make. Plus, with Dominic's gang of teardrop tattoos and deadly stare, I just knew that he was strapped. Homie was vicious; I could feel it.

"We have to figure out a way to get the kids out of the house before we do anything," Camisha advised. "We need to catch her when she's alone. See, I do have a little heart. Right, babe?"

She and Dominic shared in on the laughing.

"Well, tonight is the perfect time to get it done," I said, ignoring the last part of her sentence, ready to get this shit over with. "They're gone with Dahlia's cousin, Daphne to some recital. After that, they'll be spending the night, too." I looked over my shoulder. I'm not going to front; I was a little afraid. I'd never been involved in something like this, and I never thought I would be. Crazy what love and money could make you do. I mean, it is the root of all evil.

Dahlia and I hadn't had much to say to each other since I confronted her about Robert. She went up those stairs and never came down. Then, out of nowhere, hours later, she texted me and told me that Daphne was on her way to pick up the kids, as if we weren't in the same house, steps away from one another. I saw them off, then I left. We didn't address the elephant in the room, but did it even matter? I was more upset because I felt played. I honestly couldn't care less about her seeing someone else. I didn't know how I felt, to keep it all the way real. This was weird. Probably because I couldn't imagine Dahlia ever doing that to me—to us. She always seemed to be solely about her work and her family. That was it. Sure, things hadn't been peachy between us lately. But she hadn't given me any inkling that she was just as much over the relationship as I was. I was just trying to stick it out because I thought she loved me, and I thought she wanted to make this work for the kids. I could've gone and told Dahlia about Camisha, but just because someone else shows their hand doesn't mean that you show yours. It wouldn't change anything. And maybe it was best that I kept it to myself. She didn't need to know about Camisha. It really wasn't any of her business, since she hadn't made Robert any of mine.

"Before we go any further, are you ready for this? Are you sure you're all in? You're not going to get cold feet, are you?" Camisha rubbed the side of my head. Her craziness was attractive. I tilted it away. "Don't be acting like that. You shouldn't have any reservations. Look at what that bitch is doing to you."

"I can't believe she was cheating on me."

"Well, believe it. This is exactly why she deserves whatever is coming to her," boasted Camisha, tracing my jawline with the back of her fingers. Dominic wasn't saying anything; she was doing most of the talking.

Once I'd opened Camisha's text that she'd sent to me

earlier, I hit her with so many questions that one would think I was an interviewer. She said she'd seen Robert and Dahlia coming out of the Hotel Finial near downtown Anniston. That was right over from where the appreciation banquet was being held for Dahlia, at the Anniston City Meeting Center. Literally, it was in walking distance. Robert had also been working at that hotel for the past year or two, so she knew exactly where to find him. Trifling. And she had even gone there two or three times with his ex-wife, Jamie, when they were married. Jamie had a thing for bringing him lunch on his job, and since Jamie and Dahlia were so close, they were around each other a lot. Which meant that they just about went everywhere together. Dahlia would never do the same for me. The closest she ever came to bringing me lunch was having a pizza delivered to the plant on my birthday. And she only did that because my co-workers asked her to.

"It's eight o'clock. Time is ticking," I rushed, looking over my shoulder... again.

"Babe, the night is still very young. It's only eight fifteen. Relax," Camisha comforted. "What time does she usually go to bed? What's her routine?"

"She starts preparing for bed a little before eight, runs a bubble bath, sits in it and washes her hair for a while, then she's out by nine. She was about to get in the tub when I left."

"Hmph." Camisha jerked her neck, every detail of her face flushing.

"Hmph, what?"

I could feel her eyes on every inch of my face.

"I see you know the smallest details about her. Sounds like you've been doing quite the studying."

"Of course, I do. I've known her for half of my life," I defended. "Don't start."

"I'm not starting anything. I'm just saying; you know her very well."

"Why wouldn't I?"

"For someone you claim you haven't paid much attention to in years, I just find it odd. That's all," she said, taking her long fingernail and popping a pimple on the bottom of my chin. She had the light on her phone shining on me.

"OUCH!" I yelled, grabbing my chin. "What the hell?"

"You know I always pop your pimples for you. What's the issue?" asked Camisha. "You're acting so mean toward me, Cameron. Look, if you don't want to do this, just say it. I'll do it damn myself."

"If I don't do it, none of us are doing it. Period."

"Speak for yourself. I've *been* wanting to turn that

bitch into a corpse." She grunted. "Ugh! She makes my skin crawl."

It was like, within a press of a button, Camisha had changed. Her ways were appearing so sinisterly. I was starting to think that, maybe, just maybe, this was who she was all along. Or she could've just loved and wanted me that fucking much. I loved and wanted her, but I wasn't a killer. Until now. Everything was happening *so* fast. If only Camisha hadn't found out about Dahlia being pregnant, and if only Dahlia hadn't chosen to tell me that she was through text, none of this would be happening.

Camisha was a fool to think that I hadn't been fucking my wife, occasionally, at least, though. Dahlia and I may have been at each other's throats, but we never stopped sleeping together. It kept us connected, and it had proven to be a healthy way for us to function through the chaos after our personalities would clash. Which was most of the damn time. In other words, we had sex to at least keep that part of our lives satisfied. So, intimately, we were okay. She wasn't Camisha, but she never failed at getting my dick hard for the moment. I mean, it wasn't bad; it made our days better and our communication smoother… sometimes. Well, so we thought. Hell, we were each getting nuts together and apart. This shit is even more complicated than it was when I was the only one cheating.

"Fuck we doing? I ain't got time to just sit here, Misha-Mish," her brother complained. "It's either we're getting this shit going or I'm out."

"I'm just waiting on Cameron," replied his sister. "He seems to know her every move, so we need to move accordingly."

"Let's do it in the basement. Windows are soundproof. We can dispose the body there, too."

"Great idea," Camisha agreed. "Here's how this is going to go..."

"Okay, I'm listening," I said. "Tell me."

"Damn, nigga. Calm your shit," Camisha jeered at me. "Dom is going to act like a robber and stage it as a break-in, while we're sneaking in through the basement."

"I don't want her to see me," I objected.

"It doesn't matter if she does. She'll be dead!" Dominic coldly said, a laugh leaving his lips.

"Exactly," Camisha countered. "And you want her to see that these are the consequences of being a snake-ass bitch before she takes her last breath."

"Shit, y'all doing the same thing, so shawty ain't no worse," Dominic added his two cents for the second time. "Y'all all some scandalous-ass muthafuckas."

"Shut up, Dom," Camisha dismissed. "Anyway, this

nutcase is going to hold her at gunpoint as he brings her down to us. Then... that's when the magic is going to happen."

I nodded and okayed as Camisha steadily talked about the events that were about to take place, but although I was pissed as fuck at Dahlia and needed that hundred grand, I still felt a sense of guilt for what I was about to participate in. I'd known Dahlia since we were kids. We'd practically grown up together. She used to be my best friend, someone I could never get enough of and could tell my biggest secrets to. That woman had shown me so much, and she'd gotten me up out of the hood. I can't deny; she'd done a lot for me. Dahlia had also given me two reasons to try to be the best man I could be: Kennedy and Jaxon. What they'd lose would certainly be worth more than I'd gain. But they aren't the ones who had to live in constant turmoil—feeling like shit and getting told they aren't shit by the woman they once loved. For all that Dahlia had been putting me through, maybe she deserved this. Maybe this was her karma. Maybe Camisha was right; I needed to put myself first for a change. Dahlia was reaping all the benefits. How I was raised, she could be looked at as filthy rich, rolling in dough. Anything in the thousands meant you were doing really well for yourself, and she had definitely been racking up those zeros in her bank account. If she ever left me for Robert, I wouldn't get shit. She'd leave with everything, so what does our marriage really mean if the love is gone and the money is going with it? Staying with Dahlia was the only way I'd get my cut, but, again, staying with Dahlia would also mean leaving Camisha. And I didn't want to do that. So, my options were slim to none. I didn't want to have to depend on Dahlia anymore, and if she was gone, I wouldn't have to. I'd have everything I needed and then some. With Camisha standing right by me.

My guilty thoughts were soon invaded with real life. I could see my phone lit up from the top of the dashboard. My ringer was off, and I'd silenced the vibration. Camisha continued to ramble, but I was so focused on my phone that I barely heard a word that she said. I picked it up and saw that it was a text from the unexpected: Dahlia.

Dah-Dah: *Can you come home? We need to talk. Look, I'm sorry, okay? I've been sitting here in this tub for the last twenty minutes, crying my eyes out. I love you, Cameron. I know things haven't been great between us lately, but we're better than this. Just please come home. At least, for Ken and Jax, and for our soon-to-come newborn. They need you, and regardless of what you think, I need you. Robert and I... we were a mistake. A mistake! I'll go to couples' therapy. I'll end things with him. I promise; whatever you need me to do, I'll do it. But we can't do* *anything if you continue to run away from us.*

I thought that an own-up to what Dahlia had done would prompt me to not feel so bad about what I was organizing to do to her, but that text made this shit worse. I couldn't believe that she'd apologized. I could believe it if it was coming from the old Dahlia, but the new-money, fame-driven Dahlia? That's where it threw me off. I was almost close to saying "fuck it," but then it dawned on me that this could've been another one of Dahlia's mind games or operations of manipulation.

"Cameron! Helloooo!" Camisha snapped her fingers, beating the electronic out of my hand. "Do you not hear me talking to you?"

"My bad. I was distracted."

"Well, you need to be on your shit when we get inside," she urged. "We don't have any room for fuck-ups."

"Misha sounding like one of them gutta bitches from the block," Dominic joked, each of his elbows vacationing on the shoulders of our front seats. He then cocked back his gun, causing me to jump a tad. Chills shot through my body. "Start up this muthafucka, and let's ride, Cameron."

"Wait," said Camisha, positioning herself closer to me. "Kiss me."

I kissed her, the feeling of our lips meeting again

making me excited.

"I love you," she sensually uttered, brushing across my eyebrow hairs with her left thumb. "I love you so much."

I paused, looked her in her eyes and replied, "I love you too."

CHAPTER EIGHT

CAMISHA "MISHA" ATKINS

I was glad that I didn't have to tell Cameron that our hitman had bailed on us. Shortly before I showed up to meet Cameron, I called Dominic and made him recant what he'd said to me at his house. Coming from the money angle didn't work, so I came from another angle. I told him that I was clueless about how to commit this type of crime. The last thing I wanted to do was go to prison over a simple mistake, and I told him that, too. I don't know how it worked, but it did. I guess he'd finally seen things from my point of view, because as soon as I told him I was on my way to his house, he didn't waste any time tying his shoes. This was the Dominic I was used to.

"It looks a lot less cluttered since the last time I was down here," I told Cameron, eyeing the near-empty, unfinished basement. White sheets were thrown around the floor, plastic was nailed over the windows, a pallet bed and wooden planks were balanced against the dated, concrete wall. "You must've taken the old dining set to storage?"

"I gave it to Dahlia's sister when she came down from Virginia," he said, flitting toward the non-working washing machine that should've been taken to the dump yard by now. The drum in it had gone out months ago, according to Cameron. "I wonder what's taking Dominic so long?"

Anyone would find it hard to believe that this was what was living at the bottom of such a luxurious home. They'd renovated every other area of this residence but the basement. Evidently, this wasn't an often-visited part of the house, but it was about to be the perfect murder scene.

I'd been to Cameron and Dahlia's grand abode too many times to count, but the only time I'd stepped foot in their basement was a few days before Memorial Day, when Cameron wanted to role play and chased my ass down here. He was supposed to be the naughty preacher, and I was the dirty little church girl. It reminded me of a crazy-ass book I once read; I think the name of it was *If These Pews Could Talk* or some shit like that. Anyway, at that time, it looked like an abandoned underground room filled with a bunch of raggedy shit. Now, it put me in the mind of a construction site. That same dining set he'd passed off to Dahlia's sister was the same one he'd fucked me like a dog on. I remember how cold the pine felt against my ass and how with every insertion, the meat on my back rolled up and down the table. My cheeks were clapping against his pelvis so hard that I could've sworn I heard someone say "Hercules." We wanted to spice things up, and that was one of the best nuts he'd ever given me. Not that the others weren't record-worthy. Mr. Dargan had done a great job at pleasing me. It had to be the dick that was detaining me. Shit, maybe it was that for Dahlia, too.

"You have to ease your way into stuff like this, Cam." I laughed at how wet-behind-the-ear he was seeming. You'd think I'd done this before, but I hadn't. I just watched a lot of crime shows and paid a lot of attention to my brother's conversations with those street-roaming shooters he chilled with from time to time. "Let's give him a few more minutes."

"What is he doing?" Fiddling with the sleeves on his lime-green button-up, Cameron couldn't keep still. If he wasn't toying with himself, he was toying with something around him.

"Hell if I know?" I carelessly grabbed a piece of black art from a cardboard box full of antiques, which was trimmed in spider webs. With right my hand folded into the bottom of my black T-shirt, I then cleared the dust from the glass face of the framed artwork. "Henry Battle?"

"Who?" Cameron deposited his hands behind his back and onto the Maytag appliance, using his palms to push himself up onto the gadget's covering. "Who's Henry Battle?"

"I thought you were a fan of his work, since you have one of his paintings," I said, adoring the gorgeous *Her Time*

Well Spent drawing in my presence. The breathtaking image featured a praying African American woman, with her head bowed, eyes closed, and hands gathered. She was dressed in black, a brown shirt made of lace lying underneath. Her puffy, bantu-knotted hair was only two or three shades darker than her patinated skin. The gold hoops in her ear, along with the cross necklace draped around her fingers, silver ring on one of them, bangle bracelet on her left wrist, and unpolished, well-kept nails, magnified just how alluring the photo was. Despite how distressed she looked. Drawings like this always had a deeper meaning, and I was blessed with the gift to know exactly what that meaning was. Pain. Something that some of us, if not all, knew very well.

When I was in high school, art was my life. I was in an art club, and I used to paint all the time. You could always catch me with a brush in my hand and a canvas in front of my face. That was before I fell in love, said "fuck college," and started living with a purpose that only involved a man. For me, art was a way of expression—it used to be. I'd often find myself painting that dream wedding and Cosby-Show type of family, with the white picket fence and an Alaskan Malamute barking up something in front of our house on the hills. Through my passion, I also studied a lot. I studied to sharpen my skills. I learned so many great things about so many great people—Henry Battle being one of them.

    Just like his other projects, this one I'd found in Cameron's basement told a story. Even without words being spoken. The figure in the painting was a woman in despair. A Black woman who, after being strong for so long, had finally reached her point of weakness. I could relate. Cameron was my weakness. I was game to put it all on the line for him. I felt like I was losing my sense of common sense; I was so gone over him. Dahlia being pregnant woke something in me up. I should've thrown him to the wind and went on about my way, but how? Once you've become used to someone or something, it's hard to let go. I don't know how many times I'll have to say that, but it's the truth. It wasn't worth me giving up on him and the potential that we had on the horizon. Dahlia would just have to go, and if I had to go to extreme measures to make sure that she did, then so fucking be it. Crazy, I know. But that's honestly how I felt. I didn't even recognize myself. I didn't recognize the woman I was portraying myself to be in this very instance. But... I liked her, a tad. I liked her for loving someone so much that she'd kill for them... literally. That's love. Real love. Gutta love. Savage shit. The realest love I've ever known. She was prepared to risk anything just to be his everything. If that isn't love, then I don't know what is.

    "Oh, that old thing?" Cameron commented,

scratching the back of his head. "Aunt Geraldine gave that to Dahlia and I as a housewarming gift, when we first moved in. We never got around to putting it up, though."

"It's such a beautiful picture. You should've." I theatrically held the frame close to my chest. "Henry is one of my idols."

"You may want to check your phone. Did Dominic text you?" Cameron's antsy ass overlooked what I'd said. "H-H-He said he'd text you when he was on his way down with her, didn't he? I haven't heard any ruckus above us."

He got down from the washing machine. Hands on his hips, he did that pacing thing with his two left feet that annoyed the hell out of me. *Just be still, muthafucka. Be still.*

"Would we, really? These walls aren't the thinnest, and the bathroom that she's in is up the stairs and down the hall, the other way," I reminded him, not a bone of fright in me. "Chill out, Cam. You're too hard-up."

"Hard-up? More like scared as fuck. If this goes bad, I'll get the worst consequences out of all of us! Have you forgotten that I'm married to her? I'd be the first suspect they look at," Cameron said, getting technical and thinking too far ahead.

"I thought you wanted to do this?"

"I do, but it's taking longer than I anticipated," he

worried. "He needs to hurry the hell up!"

"Patience, babe. Patience. Man up."

Cameron's gators were hopscotching across the cement so fast, as was his heart rate, which I could sense was well over one hundred and beating like crazy. But, soon, both of ours were. Dominic came busting into the basement door and down the fourteen wooden steps, with Dahlia in one arm and a gun the size of the other. Wearing nothing but a damp, pink towel, a tear left each of Dahlia's eyes, the water from her wet tresses dripping with every step that she took. She looked as if she'd just come out of a pool of water. Her face turned red. I wouldn't have been surprised if she'd gone to a surgeon; everything about her looked fake. Faker than the prissy little bitch she made herself out to be. The big-time designer wasn't looking so big-time right now.

"Don't make me drag you, bitch!" Dominic yelled as he yanked her for dear life. "Come on!"

"Oh, God!" she came in screaming before noticing Cameron in the far corner. "Cameron?! What is this about? Please... just let us go! Please! We have children!"

"Shut the fuck up, hoe!" I slapped the piss out of her, grabbing her by her hair. The girl from The Quarters had made an appearance. I was on one, acting like one of those ghetto bitches who Dominic loved to bring around when we were younger. "These are my rules. You play by them or else!"

Sheepishly, after standing silently for about thirty seconds, Cameron slowly approached me and said, "Correction, *our* rules."

He rested his arm across the back of my neck, with the biggest smirk on his face. I loved his dimples; they were the cutest. He was cuffing me like a hood nigga would cuff his 'shawty.' I loved when he displayed his gangster roots.

"That's right, babe. My bad," I satisfyingly said, smiling and holding his hand in mine. "Our rules."

"Cameron, what the hell are you doing? What is happening right now?" Dahlia pulled her towel around, making another effort to get away from Dominic. "Get the fuck off of me!"

The two grappled, coming to a stop when Cameron shouted. This basement was so secured that you couldn't even hear an echo, so I was more than sure that no one would even be able to hear this bitch pleading for her life.

"I'm sick of you. I'm sick of being your bitch," Cameron tensely said. "You'd be better off dead than alive, since I've felt like a widow, anyway, these last few years of our marriage."

"So, you're in on this?!" Dahlia cooed. "Please tell me this is a joke!"

"No, you're a joke. You're a whore. You're a sorry excuse for a woman. Cheating with your good friend's man? Someone who was a buddy to both of us? Such a slut," Cameron mercilessly went in. "The only reason I've stayed with you is because you're the mother of my children, you've held me down, and I felt like I owed you. But what good is me allowing you to continue treating me like shit just for you to complain about doing the things that a wife is supposed to do?"

"Complain?! What do I complain about? Huh? Answer that!" she harassingly pried. "If I complain so much, I wouldn't be taking care of your weak ass!"

"Bitch, you're weak," I added. "Don't do my man. Be careful with your words; your life is depending on them."

"Your man?!" Dahlia could've pissed on herself when I said that. "Isn't this your cousin? What type of incest shit are you sickos on?!"

I didn't respond.

"See, this is what I'm talking about," Cameron exampled. "All you ever do is try to insult me, and tear me down."

"Insult you? Tear you down? I'm the one who took you in when you got tired of living in your aunt's ghetto-ass house!" Dahlia laughed. "I'm the one who gave you clean clothes to wear and nice sheets to sleep on! Me! Me and my fucking grandparents!"

"That was then. Years upon years ago. I'm talking about now. I don't even know that woman I fell in love with anymore."

"I'm the one who got you on at Coca-Cola! But all I ever do is tear you down?" Dahlia continued to make excuses. "I may be hard on you now, but that's because I love you, and I know the man that you can be! Where's that hustle you used to have? That drive?"

"I don't have hustle and drive around you because you don't fucking motivate me anymore. Camisha does. I love her! Okay?! I'm in love with her, and I want to be with her! So, that means, you have to go," Cameron truthfully let out. He was so brainwashed! Just the way I wanted him, though. "Enough of the talking. Dominic, let's get this over with."

I smiled. Whenever I'd hear him speak highly of me it made me feel good inside. Important. Number one in a class of my own. Like *that* bitch. I kissed him on the neck, staking my claim. He liked that shit. Meanwhile, Dahlia frantically waved her hands, hoping that'd get Cameron to come back to life and remember whose life he was about to end. But it wasn't working.

"I'm carrying your child! Are you for real? Cameron!

How could you?" she wailed, falling to her knees and begging for her livelihood. Dahlia seemed brittle, as if her whole world had been torn apart. *Join the club*, I wanted to say. Now she knew how I felt every time she'd done something to interfere with the one I had been revolving around Cameron, her "husband."

"My child?" He chortled. "You mean, Robert's."

"Exactly, babe. And, yes, he's for real, bitch. Him and I are getting you out of the way so we can start our life together," I provoked. "You've had yours long enough with him. It's my turn. It's my turn to get something I should've been had, if you ask me. You're nothing but recycled trash."

"And she isn't my cousin, Dahlia. I'm ready to come clean," Cameron stepped in. "I've been seeing her for quite some time, and as I said, I'm in love with her. I only told you she was my cousin so you wouldn't suspect anything."

"So, this is what it's all about? You're trying to leave me for this fat tramp?!" She talked bravely, as if a gun wasn't stamped into her Garnier-shampooed scalp. "Wow! I could've just left you alone, but you choose to kill me to get rid of me?! Why not just let me walk away?"

"We're going to be walking away with that insurance check," I gloated, rubbing the tips of my fingers together. "That big, fat insurance check, hoe!"

"You wouldn't have walked away on your own, and

you know that," said her soon-to-be ex-husband.

"So, you're really that hungry for money, Cameron? Like hell I wouldn't have! What do you offer me to make me want to stay in this marriage that bad? You're gaining everything, and you got this bitch reaping some of it, too! You know what, Camry?!" Dahlia purposely messed up my name.

"Camisha!" I made the correction.

"If you want him, you can have him!" she extended. "This man has run up my bank statements enough! It'd be a blessing to end this marriage and just go on about my life! But you know why I don't want to? Because I still care about him! That's why!"

She'd contradicted herself two times in the last sixty seconds. Neither her or Cameron could make up their mind on who or what they wanted.

Cameron was quiet. He could barely hold eye contact with Dahlia, but she couldn't break hers. The upper half of her body was covered in mascara marks. Mascara that she'd been crying off since she'd gotten down here. She was just as weak as what she clowned him for being. Bitch couldn't even hold it together long enough to get him together. Had that been me about to get my brains blown out by someone, in front of my husband—the one who set this up— I would've been talking so much shit that he would've been shut my ass up. But Dominic wasn't going to shoot until Cameron had given him the okay.

"Talk to me, Cameron! And stop letting Star Jones speak for you!" She sat her butt on the back of her legs, which were folded underneath her. "I want to hear the truth! I deserve that much!"

"Will you just go ahead and let me put her on mute? Pahhhlease! Gaaahdamn," Dominic bleated. "By the time I do shoot this hoe, I'll be 'bout dead myself."

I laughed. Dominic was pure comedy.

"I've told you the truth. Camisha has been there for me in ways that you couldn't be. A marriage is more than just sex and money, Dah. The love seemed to have left us quite a while ago." Cameron did as Dahlia said, which was to "stop letting 'Star Jones' speak for him." It was apparent that I was the 'Star Jones' she was speaking of.

"There for you in ways that I couldn't be?" Dahlia giggled. "Like what? I just find it funny how you're just now bringing this up!"

"She has not once ever made me feel less than a man for not being able to do what *she* wants me to do. Ever since I lost my job, things have taken a huge turn in our relationship. But, even before that, you've always felt like you could control me with your purse straps."

"Control you with my purse straps? Now you're sounding remedial." Her giggling continued.

"See what I mean? You don't respect a damn thing I say. So, how could you say you love me and you care about me?" Cameron walked up to her and Dominic. He then kneeled down, eye-to-eye. "This is exactly why, once your ass is dead, gone, and good in the ground, I'll be happy to cash that check. You owe me this shit, for all of the pain and suffering I've had to put up with while staying married to you. What happened to the woman I met? Now, you're just another flunky for the rich folks."

"Fuck you!" she whined as Dominic roughed her up. "I gave you two kids! One kid is in my tummy! And this is the fucking thanks that I get?! I loved you, even if I had a funny way of showing it. I fucking loved you, Cameron! I sometimes loved you more than myself! But I guess that just wasn't enough, hmph? You wanted this black bitch instead!"

"Black bitch?! Who the fuck you think you're talking to?" I checked her.

"You, bitch! I'm talking to you!" she retaliated.

Quicker than the cook time on a hot bowl of Top Ramen, something softened in Cameron. He looked at me, then at Dominic, and back to Dahlia. He couldn't do it. He couldn't stand here and watch Dahlia's murder, with his unborn inside of her. He closed his eyes and a tear rolled down his cheek.

"I can't," he told Dominic, refocusing his eyes on him. "I can't do this. Let her go."

"What? Yes, you can!" I rallied. "Don't let her trick you into not doing what's best for you!"

He trudged over to me and whispered, "She's the mother of my children. I just can't. Something in me won't let me."

I didn't say a word back to him. Instead, I simpered at Dahlia, who was grinning as if she'd won the Georgia lottery. There was a long period of odd looks being exchanged. Some more than others.

"See, I told you... he wouldn't," Dahlia said, getting up from the floor once Dominic let her loose. She let go of her towel and revealed the purple sports bra and boy shorts that she had been wearing the whole time. "I knew he wouldn't go through with it."

"Hey, you were right. I should've believed it." A few cackles left my mouth. "He's too pussy to ever do such a thing. Guess I can stop playing along now."

I sighed, picking through the edges of my hair.

"What?" Cameron gave me a perplexed look, clutching his waistline with both hands. "What did you just say, Camisha?"

"You heard me."

"I wouldn't go through with what?" he asked like a dummy. *Men.* There's a reason why they say they go to Jupiter. *Eye roll.*

"We knew you wouldn't go through with killing me," Dahlia answered, accompanying me on the other side of the room. "Aw, you actually do care about me. In some way. But it's good to know how you really feel about me. I'm a sorry human? Really, Cameron? That was low."

"*We*? Who is we?" Cameron asked suspiciously.

"Us," Dahlia took her two fingers and motioned between us. "Me and my sweet thang, Camisha."

"Sweet thang? The fuck you mean your 'sweet thang?'"

"Exactly what she said, Cameron," I supported Dahlia's statement, then gyrated toward her and stuck my tongue in her mouth. With her lips suffocating mine, we made out for a good ten seconds, getting Cameron excited with every tongue twirl and lip lock.

This had been coming to Cameron for quite a while now. Dahlia found out about me some months back. What Cameron thought she was in the dark about had already come to the light. His ass was the one still in the shadows. Funny thing is, I was actually masturbating to her husband's dick pictures he'd sent to my phone when I received a call from her. It was a Georgia area code, so I didn't think anything of it. I usually don't answer numbers I don't know, but something told me to answer this time. I did, and true enough, it was her.

When Dahlia called me, she told me that she'd found out about the affair that Cameron was having with me and that she wanted to "get to the bottom of it." I then took it upon myself to own up to the fact that I knew about her all along, but I was hopeful that Cameron would get the divorce he kept promising me he would get. That's when I let the cat out of the bag and kept it a buck with her. She could barely mumble a word when I broke it to her that Cameron and I had been seeing each other for seven years. She told me that things had been strange between her and Cameron for some time, but they never brought up the option of divorce. Then she started blaming me, saying that I was more than likely the reason behind their disconnect. I set her straight and spilled everything Cameron had been spilling to me about her—that she was a stuck-up bitch and how she had let that money and the expensive shit go to her head. At first, I couldn't take the bitch, and she couldn't take me. But we both shared something in common: the hurt that Cameron had caused us, which was the one thing that brought us together.

After Dahlia confronted me, we became a team. #TeamTakeCameronDown, that was us. He'd fucked us both over in the worst way. IE: cheating on his wife in the home that she bought and leading his side chick on to believe that they'd someday be a party of two knowing damn well that this was always going to be three's a crowd type shit. So, we wanted payback. Almost an hour post cursing each other out on the damn phone the day that she called, we came to the conclusion that dollars would always be worth more than dick. I was so mad at Cameron, for stringing me along, and Dahlia's persuasion worked. Although, I should've been blaming myself for actually thinking that a man would buy the whole cow when he could get the milk for free.

"Camisha and I have fallen for one another. Isn't this just great? Super? Ironic?" Dahlia sarcastically said, bringing her hands together for a loud applause.

Dominic and I began applauding as well.

"Fallen for one another?!?!" Cameron's nostrils were opened so wide that I could probably stick my fists through both of them. With every rise of his chest, I could tell that he was enraged and full of bafflement.

I played his ass well—like the fucking violin I used to play in the school band—and I was happy about that shit. Well, *we* played his ass. Served him right. Yeah, I know what you're thinking. *What the hell just happened?* And the answer to that is: something that needed to. Pick your face up off the floor, and while you're at it, grab Cameron's too. Shit happens; people eventually get what's coming to them.

Dahlia came up with this master plan to get Cameron back for what he'd done, and she used those dollar signs to talk me into being the one to help her see that plan out. She promised me twenty grand if I assisted in terrorizing him. She just wanted to hurt him, make him fearful, but I felt like, if we're going to go that far, we might as well go the whole mile. He needed to be dead. My thought was, why pay me out of your own wallet to help you when, if he's deceased, we could just take it out of the insurance lump sum? She was surprised that I knew about the lump sum, but there was hardly ever anything Cameron didn't tell me. It took me a minute to get her to co-sign, but once she did, she was all in. Something was fishy about that, though. You go from being a scorned wife to now a psychotic bitch? Helping to conspire your husband's murder? You'd be surprised what a couple of commas could make one do. Of course, she was going to get her cut, but I didn't understand why. She's got a hundred bands and then some sitting at Regions as we speak, so why would she need it? Eh, I said I wasn't going to be greedy, though. The bitch better be glad I was kind enough to divide it, and she wasn't as bad as Cameron made her seem. Also, she was pretty good at eating pussy, too.

I don't doubt that Cameron felt confined in his marriage to Dahlia, and I don't doubt that she changed up on his ass the moment she got some bread. But I also don't doubt that Cameron lied to Dahlia about still loving her only to keep living off of her. It may have been more so about that than the kids, which he'd been putting the blame on since I'd gotten sick and tired of being sick and tired. I knew that Cameron had lost his job way before he grew enough balls to break the news. Dahlia had let me in on that secret the day she called my phone and wondered if the money he was getting from her for "gambling" was really going to me. I confirmed that he'd been paying my bills and shit, but I wasn't too sure if those were the same funds. That was soon affirmed by Cameron when he finally decided to tell the truth to me yesterday, while we were meeting up near the AutoZone. He, at least, had been honest about Dahlia helping him get on his feet in the beginning, but he had conveniently left out the part where she'd gone back to being his money crutch. Dahlia said it herself; she was the one bringing home the bacon when they first got together. She also said that, financially, they were good until he parted from Coca-Cola. That's when he basically went back to his bummy-ass ways, and that's also when he wanted her to do everything that she was doing for him before he started working there. Personally, I don't think their problems started there, though.

    Dahlia was a ruler; she'd been ruling their marriage for a minute. And Cameron finally thought about putting his foot down. But Dahlia's argument was that she didn't take him from a boy to a man for nothing. She'd gotten a little older and a lot wiser and caring for a man wasn't anywhere on her itinerary. As she told me, 'that was for the broke little bitches.' Hell, I don't fault her. If I made as much money as she did, I wouldn't be so quick to share it either. Even though they were married, it still should've been fifty/fifty, but from what she says, Cameron wanted it to be seventy-five/twenty-five. Again, from what *she* says. He wanted an enabler, which I could see why, because the loss of his job depressed the fuck out of him. She could've been lying too, but it didn't matter.

    All that mattered was that I wasn't the one about to get the short end of the stick this time around. I could give a fuck about Dahlia and Cameron's relationship now, but after I'd been enlightened about everything, I no longer did and still don't. When Dahlia called me and told me what it really was, I realized that none of this shit was worth it. I'm not going to hold you; I was in love with Cameron's ass for seven whole years. That part was true; it wasn't a lie. I played second because I was optimistic about being put first in his life one day. But I soon comprehended something I should've been comprehended long ago: that day would never come. He was another nigga who wanted to have his cake and eat it too. He'd forever straddle the fence, if we let him. Cameron had too much to lose with Dahlia. He may have loved me, and maybe even more than Dahlia, like he'd claimed, but not enough to leave Dahlia. He thought that he could keep both of us wrapped around his damn finger, but shit started to blow right up in his face when we pulled that pregnancy prank on his ass. He's so gullible, and that made this much easier.

If I couldn't walk away with Cameron's love, I'd at least walk away with his riches.

"Fallen for one another?! Are you serious?!" Cameron had been bamboozled, and it was written all over his sweaty-ass face.

"Just like you said I'd be better off dead, Camisha and I would be better off alive... and together," Dahlia proved her point, pulling her breasts up in the bra cups. "She's the person I never knew I needed."

"Together?!" Cameron was acting as if he couldn't understand what was clear English in front of him. "The hell is going on?!"

I'd done quite the "experimenting" with Dahlia since

becoming official 'sister wives' and partners. Shit, I was vulnerable. And she was too. She told me she was curious and thought I was attractive. We were sorting out the details on how we would go about taking Cameron down when she kissed me out of nowhere. I ain't never been into the same sex, but I let the bitch eat me out a few times; that's as far as it had gone. That's why it confused me when she called me her "sweet thang" and said some shit about us being together. She was cool, and we had some fun times, but I think I liked the other side of the fence better. When she started pricking me with her nails while fingering me, I knew then that it wasn't for me. Plus, women are too gentle. I like it rough, which her husband was very good at being.

"Don't play stupid now, Cameron," Dahlia replied. "You think you're so smart, but you weren't smart enough to see what was being done?!"

We both laughed loudly. Dominic was still by the staircase, turning up the Budweiser he'd probably stolen from their refrigerator while 'acting' like he was ambushing Dahlia.

"You bitches are working together?!?!" *Wow, he finally got it.* "The fuck!!!"

Cameron almost charged at us but was stopped once Dominic pointed the head of the gun at him.

"I don't think you want to try that, my boy," Dominic

threatened. "I ain't trying to blow your fucking heart out yet. Not until these lovely ladies tell me so."

"Yeeeettt?!?! Yet?!" He pulled a Soulja Boy on us. "Dahlia, this says what kind of woman you are. I feel sorry for that baby in your belly! Hopefully, they won't inherit your sick ways!"

"Newsflash: there's no baby!" Dahlia slapped her stomach and laughed.

Cameron had already told me about the policies, of course, so once Dahlia and I joined forces, it was nothing to take advantage of that and dupe his dumb ass into thinking that my objective was to get him to turn on her, kill her, and get the moola. That was only to throw him off; it was really the other way around. Dahlia and I put together the story about her being pregnant so that it would be believable as to why I wanted Dahlia "gone" and "out of the picture." That was supposed to be my "breaking point." I uncoincidentally checked Cameron's phone that day at their house because I knew that text was about to be sent. I never checked his phone, and he knew that. His stupid ass just doesn't think. Going through his messages? That's not me. I always played my position and held my role. All of a sudden, I start being the *Inspector Gadget* bitch? He should've known that something was up, but he didn't. I guess he wasn't as intelligent as I thought he was, because I 'sho nuff' thought that he would catch on. This was something Dahlia and I had been discussing for damn near a month or two—maybe even three. But we had to wait for the right moment. She wanted me to butter him up, do it when he'd least expect something like this to even be done. The last few times I'd had sex with Cameron, I'd hit Dahlia up right after.

"Good. Was he better than me?" she'd ask. My answer to that question was always a cute chuckle and a change of subject. I didn't want to be too rude until I got what I'd come for.

The day that Cameron had come to my apartment, following the argument we'd had about him shooting another kid up his wifey, I'd just spoken to Dahlia on FaceTime. We'd gone over how I was going to act about ten times. And I acted that shit out wonderfully. We then amped things up by staging an "affair" with her friend, Jamie's, husband, Robert. Somehow, Dahlia had gotten Robert to walk across the street with her, from the hotel to the shopping market. She said she'd stop by and make it seem like she wanted to ask him about birthday gathering ideas for Jamie. I snapped those photos and off to Cameron they went. Cameron was super egotistical, and anything that played on his pride would always get a reaction out of him. We knew that'd get him to budge even more and encourage him to continue on with everything. But we also knew that by the time we'd gotten done playing mind games on his ass, he wouldn't have the guts to see it through. He was like a slinky when it came to Dahlia; she had him by the collar, hanging from her fingertips.

Once he'd gotten the receipts of Dahlia presumably cheating on him, and he'd told me about the loss of his income and Dahlia being the checkwriter, we were certain that we'd cracked him down just how we wanted him. I was going to mention about the policy anyway, but I had to find a way to do it. So, all of that came at the perfect time. Soon as I did mention it, that gave Cameron the extra nudge we needed.

When I got Dominic to agree to killing Dahlia, that's when I told him that it was really Cameron who we were out to kill. Cameron didn't mean shit to Dominic, so it wouldn't be a big deal to get rid of him. "You sure you gon' be able to do this, Mish?" he wanted to know. He knew how deep my love ran for Cameron, which is why he asked that. For a second, it did hurt me to think about doing something like this to the man I once loved more than life, but Dahlia helped me out of that guilt.

Now, here we are. Here we fucking are.

"See, a man like you needed to be brought down a

few notches," I said to Cameron. "You've been playing with my heart for all these years. I told you I was tired of your shit! If you can't beat them, join them. Isn't that the saying?"

"I loved you, Camisha! I loved you! I loved you! I fucking loved you! Believe it or not! I really did," he chanted. "But I guess this is what I get for letting a fat bitch fuck my head up."

"Oh, so, those true colors are really starting to show, huh?"

"Looks like it," Dahlia responded to me. "Look at you, Cameron. So pitiful. You don't know what else to say, because you feel stupid, so you choose to throw jabs. Grow the hell up."

"Grow?! Dead people can't grow!" I taunted. "His ass is about to be dinner for the maggots."

Cameron wanted to beat the fuck out of both of us, but Dominic wouldn't take the gun out of his face. So, I took it out of his face instead.

"Looks like you've been feasting enough! I should've been left your ass alone!" he continued to down me.

"Give me that shit," I ordered Dominic, the glock now in my possession. "It's time for this muthafucka to go."

"Wait, wait, wait," Dahlia halted me. "I thought we were going to tie him up. You know, make him suffer? Torture him a little… first?"

"He doesn't deserve another second here with us. And, quite frankly, I'm just ready to get it done."

"You're right. Make this easier on both of us, so we can go on about our lives and live happily... with each other," Dahlia said, kissing me in a way that told me we were doing more than business. For her, this was personal.

"You love me, Dahlia?" I was curious.

"Over these past few months, I've grown to."

"Past few months? What the absolute fuck?!" Cameron had gone nuts. He couldn't contain himself. "I swear to God!"

"Do you love me more than Cameron?"

She looked at me, then at him, then back to me.

"It's a different type of love. It's weird."

"But... how can you love me when—" I came with another question.

"The first time we made love, it did something to me. I can't explain it. I've never fallen for another woman before, but it was just something about you..." she went into detail. "You made me feel... wanted."

"Wanted?"

"Yes. Something that Cameron hadn't done in a while."

"If y'all were both interested in each other, why not

include me?!" I couldn't believe Cameron had said that. But, then again, maybe I could. His freaky ass. "When did this happen?!"

We avoided his nonsense. We weren't obligated to give him answers. He hadn't given us any, so why should we?

"That's good to know, Dahlia."

"Do you love me, Camisha?" she asked, putting my hair behind my ear. "Do you?"

"I do."

"Prove it," said Dahlia.

POW, POW, POW, POW!

"Damn, sis! Did you have to do him like that?! Really?!" Dominic pumped, looking down at Cameron's dead body lying before us. There were two shots planted in his torso and the other two in his stomach. I wanted to make sure that there was no possibility of him coming back to life. "That was fucked up. I ain't know you had it in you, Mish."

Tears packed my ducts, as a smile crawled upon my face. Startled, I dropped the gun on the cement, and placed my hands on my brother's shoulders.

I looked Dominic in the eyes and said, "Sometimes, a girl's got to do what a girl's got to do."

"True shit, sis. True shit," he replied with a head nod.

Dahlia grabbed me, and we held each other.

"We did it, baby," she said.

"We damn sure did," I added, as my forehead rested underneath her chin.

TWO MONTHS LATER...

"Do you see all of this shit? Bitch, we're balling," I yelled, counting through the hundred-dollar bills in my hand. Dahlia and I were sitting on the bed in her and Cameron's old room, relishing the money we'd just gotten off of Cameron's insurance return.

It'd been a couple of months since everything had gone down, and to say that I regret any of it would be a lie. Since the homicide was made to look like an attempted burglary, Dahlia's hands came out clean. Personables were scattered across the home, and Dahlia should've won an award for the battered woman who'd been assaulted and just seen her husband get murdered. Dominic and I were gone before the cops had even arrived. Dahlia waited until after Cameron was buried to begin the process for the policy. I didn't attend his funeral because there was really no need for me to do so. What place would I have held there anyway? Dahlia had a small ceremony for him. She said her kids took it pretty hard, of course, but that wasn't a problem of mine to worry about. Since his death, Dahlia and I had still been messing around, but I set my boundaries. We weren't in a relationship. Friends with benefits, maybe?!

We said we'd iron everything else out once we'd gotten the cash off of the policy. Dahlia was still working and doing her interior design stuff. Me? Well, I was just preparing for my move. I needed a change of scenery, and once I'd gotten my share of the money, I was going to Tennessee. My cousin, Celeste, had been staying in Nashville for a while, so she'd been helping me apartment hunt. First, I was going to take me a trip and sip some cocktails on the beach, though. Out of $50,000, I could spring that. A bitch needed it.

I'm sure my bestie, Mimi, did, too. I hadn't had much contact with her since all of this had gone down. She and Jeremy had been busy caring for Jeremy's disabled mother who'd come to stay with them last month. I'd catch her up on everything when the time was right. But, for now, my focus was elsewhere.

I didn't know what this meant for Dahlia and me, but I was ready to get the fuck... asap. Too much had happened for me to stay here. I wasn't the only one who seemed to need new beginnings, though. Dahlia sent her children to Atlanta to stay with their grandparents. Maybe that was best for them, and her.

"Yes!" Dahlia took a stack of twenties and started to fan herself with it. "This is what we've been waiting on, babe."

"Girl, you're already rich. The fuck were you waiting for?" I asked jokingly.

"Hey, a girl could never have too many coins."

"You're right," I said. "So, you do know you have to give my brother his cut, too, right?"

"Twenty, right?"

"Yep."

Dahlia wasn't hurting for money like I was. She was already paid and protected, so the least she could do was pay my brother for his part in this mess. Even though he ended up not doing anything. Honestly, it was refreshing to pull the trigger myself, so I wasn't mad about that. I was still happy about him being there, though.

"I'll have it in an envelope for him," Dahlia planned.

"Good. What have you decided about the house?" I

fished.

"Eh, I've been thinking about downgrading," she said. "Since Cameron is gone and the kids are away, there's no need for it."

"I would keep it. Isn't it paid for?" I questioned, getting up off of the bed.

"It is." She was on her stomach, with her feet swinging behind her.

"So, keep it."

"I'll think about it."

"Well, while you're doing that, I'm going to go downstairs and get me something to drink. All of this paper is making my mouth dry." I laughed.

She laughed along with me. "Okay."

I headed down the stairs and went into the kitchen. I opened the refrigerator and grabbed the jug of Milo's tea from the first rack, then I reached for a cup inside of the cabinet above me.

"AHHHHH!!!!!" A glass-shattering scream came from upstairs. I immediately knew that it had to be Dahlia. I dropped my cup, shaken up by the sound. A group of gunshots followed, then the whole house fell silent.

Seconds went by. I didn't move.

"It's done," Dominic announced when he came down the steps.

"You got the money?" I asked him.

"Right here," he answered, patting the duffel bag on his hip.

I smized.

"Good. Let's go."

"You got it, Miss Savage," Dominic replied, waving the weapon around in the air. "Now, help me destroy this gat so we can go shopping."

"Thanks, bro." I wrapped my arms around him.

"Always, sis."

Within one stride, we were gone.

I got up out of that house and not once did I ever look back. Cameron had gotten burned by a fire that had been blazing for a while, and Dahlia was, unfortunately, just another bystander caught in the crossfire.

I didn't have to get Dahlia killed like I'd done Cameron, but I wanted to. I wanted to because I felt like it. And I wanted the money... fuck, I needed the money. Cameron had put me through enough; I'll be damned if I compromised for the same bitch who was semi responsible for it. I wasn't as mad at her anymore, but I wasn't her friend either. However, nothing had changed in terms of who she was and what she'd done: kept him away from being mine... and he'd let her. In my eyes, they were both just as fucked up. Maybe I was fucked up, too, but I didn't care. When Dahlia came to me about the affair, I observed and I did what I saw fit.. I was so upset with how Cameron had messed me over that I agreed to her game of conning, then I turned around and conned her. What she didn't know was... I was for self, never for her. She was using me anyway, and I could feel it. I may have been stupid in love, but I wasn't stupid when it came to life in general. I knew who was for me and who wasn't. Cameron seemed to be for everybody but me, since he could never just say fuck them other bitches. Dahlia, like me, was for self, but I was only for self because people like her and her husband had made me that way. Cameron always said he loved me, but sometimes, love just isn't enough.

  Yeah, that was dirty, but if anybody deserved a dime from him, it was me. The fuck I looked like sharing that insurance money? I pretty much knew that I was going to he-he and ha-ha with her to get her comfortable with me. Since her name was on the policy, I just needed her to be the one to get the money off of it, then it was going to be 'to hell with her ass.' Just like it was to hell with Cameron. Catching feelings for him was the most horrible thing I could've ever done, so I had to end that shit. Even if it meant ending him. It was either let go or get dragged, and I was over getting dragged. I'd wasted seven years on a man, only for him to still treat me like appetizer and continue choosing someone else as his entrée. I was doing wifely duties for a man who never intended to be my husband. Somewhere along the way, common sense found me again.

And, boy, am I glad that it did.

The End

~ REACH ASHLEY TE'ARRA ~

Twitter: @ashleytearra

Instagram: @authoressashleytearra

Facebook: Authoress Ashley Te'Arra

JOIN HER OFFICIAL FACEBOOK READING GROUP!

Kickin' It with Ashley Te'Arra

CPSIA information can be obtained
at www.ICGtesting.com
Printed in the USA
LVHW041704240120
644725LV00002B/385